Just Call Me Confidence

by

Stella Grae

This is a work of fiction. Names, characters, places, and incidents are either the product of the author's imagination or are used fictitiously, and any resemblance to actual persons living or dead, business establishments, events, or locales, is entirely coincidental.

Just Call Me Confidence

Cover Art by *Kristian Norris*

The Wild Rose Press, Inc.
PO Box 708
Adams Basin, NY 14410-0708
Visit us at www.thewildrosepress.com

Publishing History
First Edition, 2023
Trade Paperback ISBN 978-1-5092-4822-3
Digital ISBN 978-1-5092-4823-0

Published in the United States of America

I have seen him at swim practice before. He is blond like Travis, but taller, thinner; he hides his blue eyes and dimples behind thick, darkly framed glasses and bangs that fall to one side of his face, nearly hiding it.

I am sitting beside the basket of kickboards, and he struts over close to me, grabbing up an armful. I sense someone staring at me and as I look up at this man our eyes lock and he smiles at me…a smile and a moment I simply cannot drive out of my mind.

Without his glasses, I swan dive into his beautiful, confident blue eyes. And he continues staring, bundling up the kickboards in his arms all while devouring me with his sexy grin, even after I stupidly let my eyes dart away from our electric communication.

At the end of practice, our eyes tangle again and I fixate on him; he looks away quickly, surprised that I give game. Without knowing anything at all about him, I know he is the kind of man who doesn't mince his words, but is gentle; the kind who takes control of the room and of any situation; he is the kind of man who sparks a wildfire in me from which I simply cannot abandon; the kind of man I decide, then and there, that I simply must have. And, there is clearly a spark between us—pheromones, errant molecules, an involuntary, uncontrollable collision between souls, the two of us picking up on the same erotic vibe—whatever is to blame, it's an inexplicable passion between strangers that can usually only be satiated one way.

Dedication

To the man who gave me my confidence—and I'll never give it back.

Chapter One

Confidence and Experience

I hold my breath and walk into the club. My skin swells with goose bumps and I hear the catch in my own nervous voice.

Inside these four walls I could meet my fantasy, my desire, and maybe even my destiny. Or, maybe just a really good time—just for tonight. I can do whatever I want to do because tonight, I'm free—in so many ways.

The bass pumps through my body while I scan the men and women, grinding in slow motion waves. A fever breaks out all over my body with a sudden mist of sweat collecting in the small of my back and between my breasts. *I want that to be me.*

My mind suddenly takes a Debbie-Downer side trip: *Am I still young enough, hot enough, and savvy enough to start over?* I know I'm not the prettiest woman out there, but that's not what entices a man and keeps him coming back for more. It's strength and substance, and those can only come from confidence, which is derived from experience. I have interesting sports stories. I can intelligently discuss, and have an opinion about politics, economics, and social issues. I'm educated; I have a real job. I've traveled, and I can cook. I've had a wide variety of experiences, which makes me *interesting, and sexy-as-hell confident.*

Of course, it doesn't hurt that I can screw without hang-ups, unlike many of my younger sisters-in-arms. And apparently, that makes me *hot*, especially to the under-thirty-and-male crowd.

The guys here are too young to understand the difference, though, but I think, *that's kinda liberating...no explaining my past, no worry about the future. It's all about the here and now. YOLO...*

I laugh and smile, getting a secret thrill out of the college-aged guys sitting behind my friends and me, rubbernecking on us. *Keep the drinks coming fellas, maybe you'll get lucky, and you'll definitely go broke trying.*

The bold brown-haired clown of the group struts over and sizes me up.

"You dance? Looks like you've got a dancer's body."

"I am. I'm a stripper," I answer him deadpan. My lady tribe cat calls and takes a shot in my honor.

He grins like a kid in trouble and my knees get a little wobbly. He keeps going, "I got nothing against strippers. You wanna dance?"

As I follow him to the dance floor, my heart pounds and my hands sweat like a silly sixth-grader at her first school dance. He comfortably wraps his arms around the small of my back and slowly lets them melt around my ass. In the shadows of the spotlights, he studies my face. The beer on his breath frames his very friendly mood. As the twenty-something female crowd picks up, his hot stare lingers on me—curiosity, admiration, forbidden territory.

With my lacy black bra playing peek-a-boo with him, his eyes hunt my neckline down to the deep V of my shirt. Smiling, he curiously quizzes me. "So, what are you and your friends doing here? Kinda looks like you might be celebrating something?"

I lock my fingers around his firm biceps, giving them a promising squeeze before I respond. "Yeah, we're here celebrating my divorce."

"Really?" He draws his head back from my face, trying to choose his words very carefully. "Do you have kids?"

"Yes, three of them—boy, girl, boy."

"Wow! You don't look old enough to have three kids, not at all. You're a MILF!" He drags my pelvis into his and grinds into me to the funky rhythm of the song. I jam my tits against his chest and tighten my stomach, wanting to be as close as possible to him. His brown eyes are clear and full of mischief. *Should I take him home with me for the night? My new dildo would probably be a better bet…I know I promised I wouldn't jump into anything—anything serious was what I meant, of course.*

"Did you call me a MILF?" I wonder out loud to him.

His infectious, teasing grin makes me giggle. He leans into me, explaining, "Hell yeah! You know what a MILF is, don't you?"

I shrug my shoulders in feigned ignorance. *Say it! I want to, I need to hear it.*

"It's a mother I'd like to fuck. A woman who has kids, but you wouldn't know it—and you don't care—because she's so damn hot. Like you. I'd absolutely *love* to have you," he whispers in my ear, letting his gaze drip all the way down my body, his fingers sweeping up and down the nape of my neck.

"Is someone keeping your kids for a few hours or

for the whole night?" His hands rhythmically knead my skirt up to mid-thigh and I let him gently pry my legs apart with his foot.

My panties are not simply wet, but unable to absorb any more of my anticipation, and I slide my calf up the opposite leg to smooth away the drip that rolls down toward my ankle. With his thumb on my clit, a finger in my pussy, and a pinky playing with my ass, I wonder, *who can see us? Is anyone watching?*

Who cares? I decide. *This feels too good to stop for something as trivial as voyeurism, and...I need this.*

His hard bulge powers his grinding, pumping his fingers deeper and more intensely into me. As my eyes gravitate up to his, I stare at him, and he watches me concentrate on his finger play. His lips fall softly on mine and his tongue snakes its way into my mouth, penetrating and pulverizing my resolve to be patient for that perfect man—perfectly right now might have to do.

As the tempo of the song quickly explodes, I pull away from him and he kisses his wet thumb, putting it to my lips; it is so sweet for so many reasons. Weaving my way through the throng of people trekking to the dance floor, I'm startled when the quiet blond of their group slips his number in the back pocket of my skirt on my way out, mouthing, *call me.*

My face aches from smiling so much. I think tonight proved something I've forgotten about myself. When I get a whistle or a double-take, or even a lingering look, I know I cannot deny it: For better or worse, I still have it. *Just call* you, *huh, baby? Just call* me *confidence.*

****

I should just go to bed, but I hold my breath and walk to the mailbox.

My neighbor is walking his dog…at nearly two in the morning on my quiet Kinweld, Tennessee street. *He thinks I'm batshit crazy, out this late, checking my mail.* I have a good reason, though.

Inside this metal tube holds my fantasy and my desire…my destiny.

I uncurl the edges of the manila envelope—C.S. Bishop, Attorney at Law—and hold my divorce papers, and really, my freedom—free from a man's expectations, free from babysitting a drunk, free from the bi-polar existence I had to fake a smile through for way too many years. For the first time since my formative years at Kinweld Community College, I am happy (and very excited) to be alone. *I sure don't plan on being lonely, though.*

I bloom inside and know that if the lube I ordered online doesn't get here later today, I won't worry because I definitely won't need it. Then, I pull the rectangle package out of the mailbox and run toward my front door, my gobsmacked neighbor wrenching his neck under my porch light, trying to get an eye full of me bouncing braless back into the house in the dark. His head would explode if he knew why I was running, or what was in the box. *Grrrrr…I tease myself…bad girl party of one.*

I tear open the box and behold my brand new deliciously large dildo—Big Blue. It's a bright sapphire blue and glittery, reminding me of my college colors. College life was much easier. At the time, I could have never convinced my young brain of that, and not that I would have wanted to. *But this…this is so much better. I'm older, not dead.*

Big Blue goes under the covers, helping me on the

road to my recovery. I grin again, remembering the brown-haired clown and how drunk I feel (not just from the alcohol), but from the *experience* of finding my way to start over at 40. Experiences certainly shape who we ultimately become—all kinds of experiences, which gives a lot of us all kinds of confidence...to make more experiences.

I let this recent memory roll into fantasy and in short order, it's like a bomb explodes inside of me, rocking me with a hundred thousand volts of lightning that percolate through me.

I strip down and jump in the shower, remembering the number the blond hottie stuffed in my skirt pocket. *To hell with the past. I've got a hell of a future.*

Chapter Two

I Love Your MILF Cougar Ass

I know better.

I *know* I know better. And to make matters worse, I'm *old* enough to know better: to understand the possible consequences of letting my pussy think for me. But I have enough experience to understand that some things only come around once in your life.

Like a hot, young stud—really hot and really young.

Summers have never been boring, but not especially exciting either, until this summer when I start the kids in swim lessons at the Kinweld Swim Club. He's little more than a kid himself, dressing the part of an old man—long sleeved, open crumpled oxford, swim trunks, and tennis shoes with black socks. With a goofy grin slathered on his face, I approach him, intrigued.

"Hi. I'm Jenna, and this is Jacob. Are you the Eel instructor?"

"Yeah, I'm Travis."

I've never been the type to be easily stirred by a man's looks. I settle Jacob in the duck row of kids and shake my moneymaker for all its worth as I find a seat in the eagle's nest of the bleachers where I can watch this magnificent piece of momma eye candy.

I can always appreciate a handsome man, but there is some otherworldly, snatch-drenching attractant certain guys have that has always been the selling point for me. This man is so hot that it burns my retinas to look at him; he should wear a warning. He's not super muscular, but athletic. As he peels his shirt off, I stop and indulge in his strong arms, tightly defined biceps, and broad shoulders. His blond hair and blue eyes pop against his tanned skin—not a tanning bed-metrosexual tan, but a beach tan, a tan that is acquired through wild, frivolous pursuits. He absolutely glows. A dragon tattoo that stretches across one side of his ribcage tells me that he could be a bad boy, but not too stupid to understand the importance of being able to hide the tat if necessary.

Over my *Glamour* magazine, I greedily spy him running his hands through his dirty blond hair, cutting up with the chubby, homely lifeguard who obviously is thinking what I am, but without the tools to make it happen—too bad for her, but great for me. *Youth is not always an advantage; confidence can trump a few wrinkles.* I whip out my phone and send myself a reminder to anonymously gift the lifeguards with some doughnuts—extra sprinkles.

With his sparkling blue eyes, he bends down on one knee, right at Jacob's four-year-old level, asking, "My name is Travis. What's your name? Are you ready for swim class? We're going to have some fun in the water!"

Immediately, I like this guy. First, he understands the importance of developing an instant rapport with his young students. Second, he's hot. Third, as I watch him with the kids—making conversation, splashing with them, encouraging them—I realize that not only does he enjoy his job, but he's really excellent at it. In the three months that *I* had tried to teach Jacob to swim, I never got much beyond the rigid limbs and screaming protests.

In less than fifteen minutes, Travis has Jacob (willingly) bobbing his head under the water, jumping in feet first, and completely comfortable and happy. Finally, the most important point, which is absolutely worthy of repetition: he's smokin' hot!

I'm in a drunken stupor, a euphoric Xanax-induced sex hangover after checking him out for forty-five glorious minutes of an otherwise mind-numbing kiddie swim lesson. I look around to size up the other moms— dirty, messy hair; no make-up; sloppy, mismatched gym clothes; totally absorbed in their mommy talk. Am I the only one who can see his hotness? God, I hope so. I smile to myself. *Glad I slipped on my ass-skimming cargo shorts and wedge sandals, and took the time to slap on some make-up.*

After the lesson, he sends Jacob my way with a friendly wave and smile. I saunter over. *Keep your abs tight. Don't miss an opportunity to flirt…it's good practice.*

"Thank you, Travis. Jacob screamed and kicked his way through the parent-child class. You must have the magic touch." I reach out, my fingers skimming his forearm.

His eyebrows arch and he pauses, reaching up to preen his hair again. He doesn't take a step backward or forward. "Yeah, he did a really good job. It'll help if you can practice with him, just to get him comfortable in the water."

"That's a great idea! Thanks for the advice. Yeah, you'll definitely see us here practicing. See you next week." I turn on my heels, shaking my ass for everything it's worth. I want to look back, but resist the urge and scurry my boy to the locker room, wet, with anticipation for the next lesson—me that is.

In all things concerning love and sex, very rarely do I make a move without advice from my best friend, Fielding Giles. As college roommates, we instantly bonded over our lust of 80s rockers and her bucket list of fuckable "old" men—Rick Springfield, Billy Idol, Bryan Adams, and (her choice, not mine) Ted Nugent. They were old to us at the time, anyway. She helped me get it on with a much older lover and then subsequently get over it—an impossible, dead-end crush I had on a man fifteen years my senior. I helped to convince her that the nerdy history geek from rural Tennessee who fell all over himself whenever he was around her, was actually very good husband material. We've been there for each other in every situation—dating fiascos, marriages, births of children, lingerie spending sprees, dirty movie screenings, my divorce, the death of her mother. My life would not be complete without her. She is the sister and the soul mate who keeps me from giving up and dissolving into a pile of useless shit.

With Fielding peering over my shoulder, I order three new appropriately slutty swimsuits and invite her over for wine and modeling.

My legs are my best asset, and my stomach is undeniably my worst. Three kids via three Cesareans is not the kindest way to treat a body, so I have no choice but to work with what I've got and make the best of it. Lucky for me, I'm vain enough to enjoy workouts and salads. I slip into an electric blue mini swim skirt and a paisley push up tankini, which covers my stomach, and dips low in the back, but still allows me to push my boobs up and out.

"Does this make you want to do me?" I ask her.

Twisting her head from one side to the other she shakes disapprovingly at me. "No. It makes me wanna ask you to bring over a sandwich."

"Dammit! That's not what I'm looking for. I need something I'm comfortable in, something that hides my stomach, and something that isn't slutty, but MILF-worthy."

Fielding throws back the rest of her merlot, rhythmically pumping her fists in the air. "Bi-ki-ni! Bi-ki-ni! Bi-ki-ni!"

"I don't look that great in a bikini."

"Oh bullshit. Try it on. Let me be the judge of that."

After several minutes of debating whether I should let her talk me into the bikini, I finally come out in a leopard print extreme push-up top and a matching bottom, with the sides tied up to *there*.

"Now *that*," she points, "makes me seriously think about boning you *and* it makes me think you're serious about wanting *me*. Of course, that point would be so much more obvious if you rubbed your tits against him."

"Do I really look okay?" Studying my stomach, I suck it in and hold it, then bend over to see what skin that's stretched its way through three pregnancies looks like.

"You're too hard on yourself. No *body* is perfect, even the models in the magazines are airbrushed. You've got a hot little body, very toned and curvy. You look like a woman, the kind of woman he's probably never had before. You know how young girls are all either straight up and down or too much jiggle and fat too soon—you've got what he wants now, and in the future. You are mysterious. Look at all the fat, lazy bitches who have given up; you make it look effortless, and he's wondering whether it really is. Trust me, Jenna. It's all about the mystery with these young guys. You could be his guilty pleasure. Besides, the majority of men want something to hold when they're getting dirty. I read that in *Sexy Madame*, you know."

"Even my little paunch?"

"Yes, even the paunch. That shit is sexy. It shows you're fertile; it appeals to his biological urges, urges he probably doesn't even know are working on him."

"That sounds awfully complicated," I grumble, smoothing down my stomach.

Fielding pats my ass. "Don't worry. Just work it."

And for the next seven weeks of swim lessons, I do.

I'm good at looking busy, incredibly occupied even, when I'm really not. I've found that gathering information—eavesdropping—during those times is the best. One of the other lifeguards asks Travis a question about going home to California. California. I *love* California. I've *been* to California—more than once, more than twice even—and I've visited cities up and down the coast. Bound to have the territory covered, I discover the opening I need to get his attention. My tits will have to do the rest in an irresistibly snug Monterey Bay Aquarium t-shirt.

Donning my white, tight conversation piece, I am thankful that Jacob is being a little turd and that I have to go over to correct him.

"Jacob! We'll have to leave if you don't stop splashing your classmates and being disruptive."

"Okay! Okay! I'll stop. I sorry, Mommy."

Travis smiles at me, waving his hand. "It's fine. He's a good listener."

His eyes dart and meet mine, then migrate to my

chest, and quickly back to my eyes. Bingo.

After class, he escorts Jacob to me, explaining, "He's doing a really good job. I can tell you've been working with him."

"Yeah, I try to get in once or twice outside of lessons."

"Yeah, I saw you here the other day."

"I saw you too," I volley back.

With an awkward pause between us, I stand up as straight as possible and spread my ribcage so he can read my t-shirt. His eyes light up and he points like a child in the candy aisle.

"You've been to the aquarium?"

With a deliberate absent-minded gaze downward, I smile. "Oh yeah, I've been a couple of times. I absolutely love it! I want to take the kids when they're old enough to make the trip and can appreciate it. Monterey was the first aquarium I ever visited; it kind of ruined me for all the rest."

"That's so cool! I grew up not far from Monterey—San Miguel."

"Isn't that close to Paso Robles?" I ask, hoping my memory of California geography is close enough to keep the spark in our conversation.

"Yeah! Have you been there?"

"I went there several years ago to visit some wineries, and ended up finding an olive farm to tour. If we weren't settled here in Kinweld, I'd move to California in a minute."

"Wow! You did all that by yourself?"

Here it is: The question that reveals a thousand subtleties:

Him: Are you single? Are you available? It's cool to

find a girl I can have an intelligent discussion with about my hometown, or just an intelligent conversation. Period.

Me: I am single and very much want to be available to you. Do we have enough in common to bridge our age difference? Then again, you're so hot does it matter?

"Actually, at the time I was married, but I'm not now. It was still a good trip, though." I smile and hold his gaze until I have to look away. My eyes find his again and he's still fixed on me. A blush creeps across my face and drops of sweat break out across the small of my back and in between my legs.

Me: Again, yes, I'm available, interesting, and I want to rock your world, if only from the waist down. I think you're making me wet!

He gives his swimsuit a quick pull n' stay away from his body; I grin at my toes, hoping it's because of me. "Well, I guess I'll see you next week, Jenna. Jacob, see you buddy!"

****

"Have you made any progress on your pet project?" Fielding quizzes me, shoveling a giant bite of the enchiladas I whipped up into her yap.

"Well, I know he's from California, so I wore my tighty-whitey Monterey Bay Aquarium t-shirt, and we struck up a conversation—a really *good* conversation."

Fielding's enchilada receives a temporary pardon from its mastication. "What? Tell me! I'm a bored married woman living vicariously through you!"

"Well, there's not all that much to tell. We talked, he looked at me, and I mean *really* looked at me, I ogled him, got turned on, came home, and masturbated while the kids watched Looney Tunes."

"So, when are you going to screw him?"

"I don't know. As soon as possible, I hope. I don't think I can last much longer just on fantasy and masturbation. But, I can't tell if he's really interested, or just intrigued."

"Listen," waving her hand, she takes another bite. "Young single guys want one of two things: to get married and settle down or to get laid. And probably, getting laid is at the top of the list, regardless of the other. You aren't ready for another relationship; you don't want anything complicated, and so much the better. You just need to let him know that."

"How do I communicate that to him without looking like a cheap slut?"

"Duh! Wear your bikinis and touch him, talk to him, smile at him. It's not rocket science. Men are pretty simple, especially the horny young ones who don't have any baggage yet."

"I think I'm out of practice," I sigh.

"Well, get back in the game. Say, can I have another one of those enchiladas?"

****

Over the next several weeks with multiple lessons for multiple kids, I'm seeing a lot of Travis, and he's seeing a lot of me. I rent a new Abs of Steel workout from the library every week for two weeks and by the third week I'm ready to showcase my three new bikinis.

Outside of lessons, I bring the kids to practice swimming, discovering that I can usually have him all to myself at lunchtime—he's the only lifeguard on duty during everyone else's siesta. Besides a few old folks, I realize this delicious secret: *I am the only MILF.*

The first day I walk in with my animal print bikini

he waves from his perch, and accidentally drops his red life preserver in the water. The kiddie pool has its own lifeguard, and the five of us—my kids, Travis, and me—are often alone. I fall back on our California dreaming conversation, and he often does something nice like offering to get a float or a swim noodle for one of the kids. Despite my best flirting, he appears more comfortable talking with the kids than with me. So, I do what any woman with the goods would do: I show them.

Every red-blooded gal who has ever worn a halter bikini top tied by her own hands has known the fear of the knot working loose. But, you figure out very quickly what knots work, and which don't. I tie one that I am sure won't stay; what goes up must come down, and, with enough rough play with the kids, I (happily) experience a wardrobe malfunction.

"Mom! I see your boobies!" my oldest yells. The other two cover their eyes and mouths in disbelief and embarrassment for me, giggling like crazy. Freud would probably have words for me…a complex oedipal mix of words that would keep me up at night.

As quickly as I can (but not *too* quickly), I pull my halter up and give a convincing show of embarrassment, letting my eyes circle up to him. But instead of a grin to greet me, his face contorts into a horrified stupor. I think I've turned him off.

Feeling stupid and immature, I gather the kids and we go home.

Tomorrow is Friday and my ex has the kids. After the first aid class I have to finish on Friday night at the club, I'll have the weekend to regroup and rethink my whole smoking hot momma adventure.

I ask Fielding to an emergency sushi-packed lunch

on Friday and confess my transgression.

"Is it too early for a sake, and would it be *too* wrong for me to go back to work slightly intoxicated?" she wonders out loud.

"Uh, give me a double no on that. Anyway, it's Dumb Friday. Nobody really does any work on Friday afternoons, or at least I don't. But, I've got bigger problems: I showed Mr. Young Stud my tits at the pool and he looked totally freaked out, I mean almost horrified."

Fielding slings back her sake, declaring, "Ugh, that's not good. Have you ever considered maybe he's gay? Or, maybe he's one of those little delusional boys who is saving himself for marriage?"

"I don't think I can go back to lessons. After they're over, I'm done. He's clearly not interested."

"Oh, I'm not sure you can say that for sure. Maybe he's never seen a set of tits before."

"Well, if that's the case, I don't think I want him."

"Lots of young fish left in the sea, my mature mermaid. What are you doing this weekend?"

"Well, after my ex picks up the kids, I've got to go to the club to take a first aid class."

Slamming her hand on the table, she blurts out, "Well, see! You might find a whole new piece of young stud ass that you dig even better, *and* he might actually like seeing your tits."

"I hope you're right. I need a tangible transition from my fantasy. Pass that sake over here."

****

I don't believe in fate. Life is not about what happens to you, but what you decide to do about it when you're thrown the big curve ball.

The first aid class is torture; it drags by and saps every bit of energy and hope I have for a good weekend. Not wanting to go home, I don't really have any other place to go either, so I slowly gather my things and sneak out of the classroom, giving one last regretful look toward the pool.

"Hey! What are you doing here so late?"

It's a familiar voice, but I can't bring the face into mental focus. Slowly, I turn toward the vocalist. Travis' sharp blue curious eyes meet mine.

I push our last awkward "tit à tit" to the back of my mind, and giving him my sweetest smile, I purr, "I took a first aid class. With three kids, I figure it might come in handy someday."

Silence lingers between us, but it's not awkward, or even uncomfortable. It's charged with sex; I can sense it, and so can he.

"You should probably let me walk you out to your car. It's pretty dark out there.

"Okay."

With only the buzz of the fluorescent lights he asks, "So, where are your kids?"

"They're with their dad for the weekend. I'm on my own. It's weird with the house being so quiet and empty." I slow my pace, giving him lots of time to weigh his options.

He clears his throat. "Your kids are really nice. I enjoy teaching them, especially Jacob. He's got a really cool little personality."

"Yeah, I'm lucky. They are good kids, and nice. I think you're nice, too, and really handsome, and smart. It's fun talking to you. *That's* a very cool combination."

Quickly, his eyes dart away from mine and I watch

him swallow hard. We stop in the middle of the nearly empty parking lot. With only the floodlights on us, I notice he's struggling with his thoughts, his words. I press my body up against him and push my lips to his—salty, quivering; his breath falls on my mouth with uncontrolled intensity.

"Let me make this easy on you," I whisper in his ear. "I think you're hot, and I'm not looking for a serious relationship, just fun. Do you want to have some no-strings-attached adult fun with me? I promise it will be the best lay you've ever had in your life."

"Where are you parked?"

"There, the blue van."

I hardly get the door open and he sweeps up behind me, kissing my ears, my neck, and pulling my peasant blouse down to expose my bare shoulders, licking them. My knees buckle as he grinds his hard-on into my ass.

"My place is only ten minutes away," he whispers.

"I don't think I can wait that long."

I pull him into the van and close the door. Throwing the booster seat to the front we collapse on the length of the back bench seat, grinding until we both nearly come in our pants. He's a good kisser, so good in fact, my panties are soaked before he unzips my jeans and shimmies them over my hips. As I sit up to take my top off, I remember the tit incident, and decide—for better or worse—to get down to what that was all about.

"Travis? I have to ask you a question. It's important."

He never stops kissing me. "What, baby? Don't worry. I don't have anything, I swear, I'm clean. Are you worried about birth control?"

"No, I'm on the pill, and I have condoms. It's not

that; it's the day my top came down at the pool."

"Oh damn!" he groans, reaching up to help himself to a handful of me. "That was probably one of the best days I've had at work—*ever*. I couldn't believe my luck! Some of the other guards were pissed they missed that!"

Laughing, and relieved, I drop the subject and reach down to unbutton his jeans, massaging his cock. Now, in every woman's lusty fantasy, the object of her affection always has a porn star-sized dick, and knows how to use it in ways we never knew existed, no matter how many times you've been around the block. Unfortunately, those of us who've been around the block more than once, or twice, or even three times, know this is normally the exception rather than the rule. But when it's not, it's the kind of thing you want to get on and not stop riding— ever. Fire, Biblical flood, nuclear disaster, asteroid— nothing is going to get me off of him once I get on. It really is that spectacular.

Now I know why he always checks for cling in his swim shorts after he jumps out of the pool. Can you imagine if one of those little kids saw *that*? *"Mommy, why does my swim teacher have a big lump in his pants?"* And, the moms—he'd never have time to teach, what with all the ladies hanging around to check out his jock.

"I want you inside of me. Now!" I demand, ripping his shirt up and over his head, gently biting and licking his lips. I go down on him, shoving his entire, beautiful, huge cock to the back of my throat and spanking it against the soft pillow in the middle of my tongue, which I slide up and down the shaft, not wasting any time in moving to his balls. As I put my mouth around them, he yelps, wrapping his hand around the back of my neck, pushing me back to his human lollipop.

"What do you want?" I stop, coming up for air to see the expression on his face.

"I want you to do that again, please! That felt so motherfucking good!" he moans.

"Okay, but don't come, or at least not before me. There's still a lot of fun we haven't had."

I don't wait for an answer, trusting that if he does come, like most horny young guys, it won't be long before he can be hard again and ready to go.

If there's one thing I've learned from all my experience, it's this: NEVER underestimate the power of a great blow job. I am utterly convinced that while a face may launch a thousand ships, a great blow job will compel the best captain to run that mother aground and never look back. Simply put, do *not* be stingy with the blow jobs.

He bucks and writhes under me, tensing his legs and kneading my hair, moaning in rhythm with me while I play with myself. Finally, I've had enough foreplay. I literally ache for him to be inside of me. *If I don't come very soon, I think I might sustain permanent damage to my woman parts.*

I grab his head and make him stop licking my nipples. I put my eyes as close to him as possible, never letting him leave the visual lockdown I have on him. "Travis, please, I need you to make me come! Make me scream."

I don't have to say it again.

Within three pumps, the mounting pressure in my clit releases a tsunami wave of pleasure and I attack his mouth—kissing, biting, and licking every place I can reach. I do not care who can hear me screaming and moaning, and I do not care what he thinks of my crying. For the first time in too many years, I am having the kind of sex I want: *I deserve it this good and I'm the fucking rock star of all MILFs!*

His heavy breathing and dirty talk keep winding me up. "I've watched you and wondered what it would be like to be in your tight little girl. I didn't know Mommy was such a nasty little freak. Come for me, baby! I want to watch you come!" He yanks my thigh up and throws it up over his shoulder, sliding deeper and faster into me.

I come until my legs and back are burning and cramped, and I'm sliding around on the seat from all of my wetness. Motioning for him to sit up on the seat, I straddle him, face-to-face, wrapping his baby soft hands around my tits, riding him slowly, precisely, until his breathing comes in erratic spurts; I watch him slide in and out of me, playing with his balls. His chest folds in and out as I listen to him struggle for air, then moaning.

"Oh fuck! Damn, baby!" Leaning back on the seat, he rests his hands on my thighs, keeping himself inside of me; I can still feel his hard dick throbbing. Pulling my chest to his, he drops his head and rests his face on my soft mounds, kissing my nipples.

"If you don't stop, you may be busy again sooner than you think," I warn, giving him a wink.

"That was awesome! Shit! I guessed you'd be good, but I thought you were just talking shit about the best lay of my life. That…that was bangin' hot! It was better than just taking home some bar trash to get off with, you know what I mean? Damn! I love that I can talk Cali with you!" He throws his head back and I watch his uneven grin spread as he replays it all in his mind. "I was hoping you might notice that I've been checking you out during swim lessons. You're the hottest woman at the Kinweld Swim Club. All the dudes—we've discussed you. We call you cougar panties—'Cougar panties in the building!'—you know those skimpy animal print bikini bottoms you have, your sweet ass hanging out the back? They are do-me-yummy."

"Yeah, I know those. I just didn't realize they had sparked a secret code. Come spend the night with me, or the weekend. I'll make you breakfast in the morning," I demand, my ego surging.

"What would you make me?" He asks, entertaining the idea of playing a real grown-up.

"How about chocolate chip smiley-face pancakes?" I giggle.

He flips me to my back, offering, "How about I go down on you and you fix me something else?"

"That's one of the best ideas you've had all night." I watch as he gently tickles my pink ruffles with his tongue. "And that," I point, "is one of the nicest things you could do for me."

And it is—until he introduces me to his friend Collin.

Chapter Three

Collin Out for Me

I have seen Collin at swim practice before; he is blond like Travis, but taller, thinner. He hides his blue eyes and dimples behind thick, darkly framed glasses and bangs that fall to one side of his face. He's not the kind of guy who necessarily gets a lot of second looks, or at least, I never gave him one until the night fickle fate walks him my way.

I am sitting beside the basket of kickboards, and he struts over close to me, grabbing up an armful. I sense someone staring at me and as I look up at this man our eyes lock and he smiles at me…a smile and a moment I simply cannot drive out of my mind.

Without his glasses, I swan dive into his beautiful, confident blue eyes. And he *continues* staring, bundling up the kickboards in his arms all while devouring me with his sexy grin, even after I stupidly let my eyes dart away from our electric communication.

At the end of practice, our eyes tangle again, and I fixate on him; he looks away quickly, surprised that I give game. Without knowing anything at all about him, I know the kind of man he is: the kind that doesn't mince his words, but is gentle; the kind who takes control of the room and of any situation; he is the kind of man who sparks a wildfire in me from which I simply cannot abandon; the kind of man I decide, then and there, that I simply must have.

And, there is clearly a spark between us— pheromones, errant molecules, an involuntary, uncontrollable collision between souls, the two of us picking up on the same erotic vibe—whatever is to blame, it's an inexplicable passion between strangers that can usually only be satiated one way.

Every week I anticipate his eyes roaming to find me, his desire dripping all the way down my body, wrapping it in his hot snare. We share intimate moments, both of us pleasuring the other with a tacit white hot public passion.

Usually he just stares intensely, but one night, he bird-dogs my walk around the opposite side of the pool, and quickens his pace to meet me—face-to-face—the momentum and courage building in his eyes is thick, touchable. Our eyes collide again and he softly whispers, "Hey." I give him the same. It's not much, but it is enough. *I want more.*

I yearn, watching him wind through the maze of kids arriving for swim lessons. He finds a seat in the lobby, facing the large window opening to the pool area. I can see him; he can see me. Casually, he grabs a magazine and I argue with myself: *Don't chase after him! Things with Travis are going well…but he's a boy toy—sexy, hot fun, and without a lot of cares about anything that's important to a grown woman. Basically, he's a big kid— a big, sexy kid. Okay, a big, sexy kid who knows how to screw me silly with his queen size dick. And that is definitely worth something.* The thought of Travis is still keeping me honest—and satisfied—*for now.*

As soon as my kids run over to sit at the edge of the

pool with their instructors, Travis motions me to the Special Needs locker room. There are individual rooms with doors—and locks.

We slip into one of the rooms and he latches the door, swiftly slipping off his swim shorts. Turning on the shower, he shuttles over, unmercifully yanking off my workout shorts and tank top. Our mouths melt over each other.

Pulling me into the water, he directs the shower head onto my clit, teasing me with his thumb and the tip of his hard cock, which he uses to trace every inch of my wetness. I pull my leg up, propping it on the shower wall, watching his shaking fingers struggle with the rubber. He enters me slowly, the warm water washing over us, and I am so wet, and so ready for him to make me come. With his strong hands he grapples my bottom, pushing his face against mine; we open our mouths, his lips lightly settling on mine and we rhythmically moan, funneling energy and intensity from each other.

Travis fills up my space and I am completely defenseless, splaying my lips apart with his full, throbbing bad boy. His breath comes in sprints, his pumping staccato until we both bow at the knee and come—loudly. We dress hurriedly, giggling at our naughty quickie. Peeking out the door, he gives me the all-clear signal and I scurry out to situate myself alongside the other parents.

My eyes curiously wander to the lobby again and I see Collin undressing me with his eyes. At the moment I catch him red-handed, he sinks back into his reading, pretending to be uninterested and innocent.

Listening to the sounds of splashing and giggling from the pool, I chide myself for being too much like a schoolgirl. I gather up my bags and exit to the lobby, picking a table facing his. He doesn't look up, so I walk by him to get some water. He intently flips through his magazines, hanging around, attempting to seem unassuming. I try to catch his eyes, but they never roam my way again, and finally, I give up trying to get his attention.

As the kids and I leave, I see Collin patrolling the lobby, waiting for something, or someone. My eyes quickly move his way and he watches me scurry out into the dark. A wave of desire immediately shakes me. *I want more, but not from Travis.*

The final swim lesson drags me to this forgone conclusion: *I need to be with Collin.* My palms are sweaty, my breathing is shallow, I quiver. *What the hell is this man doing to me?* I wonder.

As soon as I step out of the locker room, he is there, patrolling the side of the pool, as if he's lying in wait for me. He is in his swim trunks and shirtless; his guns are awesome, his abs are tight and luscious. I want to lick them, and follow his goody trail all the way to his crotch, and never stop licking. Our eyes wander around, trying to avoid the inevitable. We give in, crashing into each other; we playfully mingle, except his eyes greedily hoard a passion and an intensity that I've not seen in a very, very long time.

He is a *man* absolutely famished for me.

Immediately, I know: *He could have me at any time and in any way he wanted, as much as he could handle.* I know this as I know my own skin.

Trying to smile, I gulp hard and manage a meek turn of the lips, but have to look away because he's making me banging hot with the smoldering vibes coming out of his eyes. He flexes his muscles, puffing himself up, raking his fingers through his hair, all the while keeping me trapped in a visual half Nelson. I imagine his mouth on mine, tasting all my special spots, wet and desperate and hard, swooping me under him with his strong arms, trapped with all this chemistry brewing here between us, chopping my resolve to be a good girl to nothing.

Suddenly, I spy Travis out of the corner of my eye. He lumbers out of the men's locker room and waves at me. I wave back, smiling, and Collin spins around to catch Travis' hand on his shoulder. Motioning me over, I am totally unprepared to do battle with my conscience over this predicament.

"Hey, honey! How's it goin'?" Travis wraps his arm around my neck and gives me a squeeze and a quick peck on the cheek. "I want you to meet somebody. This is my friend, Collin."

Traitor. Cheater. Fraud. Liar. Although Travis and I haven't really discussed exclusivity, or monogamy, or the girlfriend title, we've certainly fallen into a convenient weekend pattern that concludes with my barely being able to walk at work on Mondays.

I extend my hand. "Hi, Collin. It's nice to meet you. I'm Jenna." When our hands cup for the shake, I tremble as his hand squeezes mine—keeping it longer than he should. I pull away; his eyes strip me of confidence and I am completely vulnerable to him. Travis is blissfully ignorant of the attraction between us.

Ignoring Travis, Collin says, "I've seen you here some. You come with your kids on Wednesdays and Fridays, don't you?"

"Yeah, I do," I meekly squeak out. He knows good and well when I'm here, and I know that he knows.

With a very serious look on his face, he continues to ogle me, and I hold steady with him all the while Travis chats away about anything and everything under the blue moon that is only truly interesting if you're between the ages of twelve and twenty. After several minutes, I don't even think I hear Travis anymore.

"Hey, babe, did you hear me? I'll call you in a couple of days and we'll plan something for the weekend." Travis winks at me and my knees turn weak thinking about our weekend somethings. I offer Collin one final, helpless look and an idea springs into my head.

"Hey, Travis!" I yell, turning on my heel to discover Collin's eyes devouring my legs. "Why don't you bring a couple of your friends on Saturday? I'll grill some hamburgers and we can watch the Tennessee-Florida game. It's usually a wicked match-up; they're playing at home in Knoxville."

His eyes light up at the thought of a free meal (and a really good one at that), a built-in booty call, *and* his friends. "Yeah. Yeah! That's awesome. Want me to bring the beer?"

"Sure, be there about noon. Just let me know tomorrow how many people are coming so I can make enough." As I turn to leave, Travis happily wanders off, looking back only once to see me waving at him. Collin's eyes rope me in again and I add, "You can come, too, you know. It's 3603 Bonaire Wood Drive."

Hesitating, he smiles. "Well, Travis didn't really invite me."

"No, but I did. He won't care. In fact, he may not even notice." We let ourselves have a quiet laugh at Travis' expense. "So, I'll see you Saturday, about ten?"

A curious grin creeps across his face. "I thought you

said noon?"

"Noon for them, but ten for you."

On my weak knees, I turn to walk over to the kids, feeling his hot stare on me. I'm not exactly sure where things are heading with Collin, or what I am going to do, but I know this: I'll be game for anything he wants to do. I can't help but be: this man and I have some seriously sexy shit brewing.

Chapter Four

Just a Woman With a Man's Morals

Fielding meets me for our usual Friday lunch—Mexican. Over margaritas, I confess my naughty cheating plan.

"That's so unfair. That is *so* unfair! You're one *bad* mamacita." In between bites of chips and guacamole, she adds, "You've got this hot boy toy with a big tool who pounds you whenever you want it. And then, you've got this hot thing happening with his friend, *and* he's just as hot?" She slaps her forehead.

"No, he's not quite as hot, on a purely physical level—Travis is basically just Momma's eye candy—but when Collin stares at me the way he does, when he gives me that look, I don't even know what the hell to call it, my panties just get so hot I think they're going to spontaneously combust and melt right off. I mean, I want to get into his pants *and* into his brain. He's smart, I can tell it, and confident. God, the confidence this guy has at such a young age. It's just...I think I'm obsessed. It's crazy! It doesn't make sense!"

Fielding stops mid-chip and shelters my hands in hers. "Are you falling in love with him? I read that in some cases it only takes like one fifth of a second to fall in love with someone."

"I don't know! I don't think so. How would that

even be possible? I hardly know him! We're just on a first-name basis. How can that be love? That's ridiculous. Maybe Travis has *finally* fucked my brains out."

She laughs and shakes her head. "Or maybe it's something else. That happened with Cliff and me, and I just knew, after you persuaded me for a semester, of course. But, I think I knew before I was really consciously aware of it. Maybe our humid Tennessee river valley summer has baked your brain. So, are you planning a ménage a trois or what?"

"Hell no! I'm just going to plan on cheating on my boy toy, if it comes to that. Collin didn't even agree to come. I put the invitation out there…who knows."

"You know, don't you? There is something going on here—animal attraction—*mojo loco*. Boom! Pow! Bam! Jenna, listen, just let me give you some advice: Be open for whatever is possible, that's all."

"I'll open my legs for it," I joke.

"Yeah, you don't have any problem doing that, do you?"

****

I can't get Travis out of my hair soon enough come Saturday morning, despite the quickie and the to-go cup of coffee. As I shoo him out of the house, he turns his baby blue eyes to me, visibly upset.

"Did I do something wrong? I was gonna stay and help you. If you tell me what to do I can help." He stands in front of me with a wounded look on his face; the same look my four-year-old gets when he's just been disciplined for something he can't yet fully understand.

Sidling up to him, I press my soft body into his and offer a long kiss. "You can help by going to get the beer and chips and stuff. Isn't that what you planned to do?"

A pang of guilt cold cocks me back into reality: *Do I really want to continue aimlessly banging Travis when I can bang Collin and actually connect with a man on some emotional and intellectual level, too? Maybe I can pull off both...*

With his crooked grin, I see he is satisfied. "Okay. I'll be back in a couple of hours, and I'll man the grill." Pulling me to him, he plants a wet, passionate kiss on my jugular. "Don't start without me," he whispers, "don't start *anything at all* without me."

I watch him screech out of the driveway and wave aimlessly from the porch in my nightgown.

As I jump in the shower to wash Travis off of me, the memory of Collin's eyes practically fucking me gets me hot. I squirt some soap in my fingers and push them against my lips, slipping back and forth between my clit and ass. I prop my leg up on the shower wall and bending over, let the water spill over my hot box, large drops gently teasing me into a frenzy.

With clean fingers, I circle my clitoris, tapping and pressing it more aggressively each time. The fingers on my other hand greedily invade my pussy, plunging in and out until my hips buck and sway with them. I push hard against my clitoris; a wave builds, as I imagine how Collin's hardness will fill me up, our tension unleashed on each other.

Quickly, I grab my washcloth and shove it full in my mouth, sucking on it, moaning, driving my fingers deeper into my hole, giving my clit the bulldozing it wants. A bomb explodes inside of me, rocking my sugar walls; my pulse echoes in my head, and I glance down to see a thin trail of white dripping down my leg.

"Shit!" I yell. I take a deep breath and stop to consider what will happen if I ditch Travis and Collin isn't interested, or if he can't deliver the passion I crave. *What if this sexy young stud is a dud?* I lecture myself.

Emotional connections and passion are built—not in a day—but slowly. I have to be willing to savor each hot, savory morsel of attention he's obviously willing to give me. *This one could take time; time well worth the effort—at least that is my bet. Just be you…confident you.*

I keep my hands busy in the kitchen: patting out hamburgers; filling dip bowls; pulling together cups, plates, and napkins. The grandfather clock in the hallway strikes ten times. I step out on the deck to sweep and pull more chairs out of the storage house.

As I bend over to pick up a stack two high, something in my back snaps and an excruciating pain follows very quickly. I yelp, but to no avail; my neighbors are not outside and I am alone. As I try to lift myself up off of the deck, I force myself back to my original position only to discover that I can either be flat on my back or I can lob myself over on my stomach. Any other position is brutal.

"Shit!" I yell, not for anyone in particular to hear, but because I am suddenly grimly aware of my age, and because I can see the clock—10:15.

For the next twenty-five minutes I flip back and forth, and at 10:40, I hear the doorbell. It's either one of my knights in shining armor, or the grim reaper. At this point, I will settle for any one of the above three.

If nothing else, he is persistent, ringing it three more times before I hear the bell fade away. Over the rattling of the lock on the side gate I hear a "Hello?" that is not completely familiar, but not the voice of a stranger either: Collin. I take a deep breath and decide that this can either be a terribly embarrassing moment that will turn him off, or I can use it as a destructively charming attempt to get physical with him. In three months we could very well be rolling on the floor belly laughing, nearly peeing our pants, reminiscing about this incident.

"Uh, I'm back here, on the deck! I've decided to greet all my guests horizontally," I quip, hoping he sees the humor in the situation.

His head eclipses the sun, facial features undefined, but he's broader than Travis, and taller. "So, you've fallen and can't get up?"

I laugh, but it hurts. "Well, I thought about subtly flirting with you for the whole party, but decided that I'd just make it obvious what I wanted."

He rolls me to my side and with his index and middle fingers, pushes and straightens the muscles on either side of my spine. "I wish I could tell you that I've got what you need, baby, but I'm fresh out of medical assist necklaces."

I guffaw and flinch, reaching out to swat him. "Oh, I think whatever you're substituting with will do just fine."

Kneeling over me, his smile is infectious, and we can hardly maneuver for an incurable case of the giggles. "Lucky for you," he wags his finger at me, "I know a thing or two about injuries. I'll be starting my medical residency in a few months. It feels like you've pulled a muscle in your back—easy enough to fix. But you'll have to take it easy for a couple of days."

"Well, that should be easy enough." I reach over to pat his face and let my hand linger against his stubble. "I knew you were smart, but gosh, not a freaking genius. Medical school is a huge undertaking."

He covers his hand over mine and lifts me over his shoulder. "This is my best pick-up move. You're lucky, most women don't appreciate it." He kicks open the back door and gently launches me on the couch. "Don't move! I'll take care of the stuff outside. Want me to pull all of the chairs out for you?"

"Yes, please do."

"See, you should have just waited until I got here!"

I twist a curl around my finger. *Should I be totally vulnerable with him? Nah, I've already blown that theory all to hell.* "I wasn't sure you'd come."

"Yeah…I wasn't either. But then I just couldn't get you and your pretty face out of my head."

A blush creeps across my cheeks as he locks his eyes on me. I am aware of my breathing—deep and purposeful, blowing through my lips—and he swaggers over.

"I hope you don't mind if I kiss you. I'm tired of just imagining how good it will feel."

He plants a sultry, determined kiss on my lips, letting his fingers trace my jaw line. As suddenly as he overtakes me, he's out the door, doing exactly what I would do, if I could—Mr. Take Control is taking over. Apparently, he's my confidence twin flame.

Collin finishes outside and I eagerly wait for the two of us to sit together—alone. He brushes his hair out of his face; he left his glasses at home and the intensity of his blue eyes crushes me.

"What else can I do to help you?" He sits close to me on the couch and grabbing my legs, puts my feet in his lap. "That better?" Running his hands over my feet and calves, he slides them up to rest on the tops of my thighs.

"I want to get to know you better. Tell me something about yourself not many people know," I request, covering his hands with mine, trying not to shiver from his touch.

"I'm scared of being alone."

I laugh, "Well, who's not? Isn't that the bane of human existence? What else?"

"I broke up with my girlfriend because it was going to eventually happen anyway—it was long overdue actually—*and* because…because I'm intrigued by you. For some insane reason, I just can't kick you out of my mind. We seem to have a little more going on than just your average case of lust. No one else knows that, except for you and me. Oh, and secretly," he whispers, cupping my ear in his hand, "I'm glad you hurt your back. Otherwise, I'd have to think of some other excuse to touch you like this."

My heart races and I have to remember to breathe. Mr. Take Control is wise beyond his years, and understands all too well that my heart is a game-free zone.

Without thinking, I blurt out, "If my back wasn't hurt, I'd so ride you right now."

For several seconds he sits expressionless, contemplating my words, imagining what it would be like, and a sly smile turns up the corners of his mouth. "You and I—we've got something here between us, but I've got to have more, and I've got to know that I'm the *only one* having it—I wanna play fair. Do you get what I mean? What's between you and Travis?"

What's between you and Travis? The question

rattles around in my brain and while I formulate an answer, I consider what cutting Travis loose could mean. "We're friends with benefits. I am physically attracted to him, but…he's not anyone I could really have a relationship with at this point in my life. He's fun, that's all."

Collin shakes his head in agreement. I'm not sure whether he's ever had a relationship like that before, but he certainly understands the sexual component. Thinking out loud he begins his laundry list of pros and cons. "He's better looking than me, and he might have a bigger tool than me," he scratches his chin, recklessly choosing his words. "So why me? How do you know you could be happy with me, or are you only interested in happily screwing with me?" He wonders out loud.

Ignoring the sharp pain in my back, I grab his shirt and pull him to me, letting him help me hoist myself onto his lap. With his face in my hands, I confess, "It's you over him because I think you're smarter, you're more mature, and most importantly, because when you look at me, you make me feel like I'm the only woman in the whole world. That's why. That's why I want you, why I want to let you have me wholly and completely." I seal my confession with a slow, wet kiss that's interrupted by the doorbell. I look at the clock—it's nearly noon. The fraternity circus will start soon.

Collin gets up to answer the door and I hear Travis' voice. "Hey man! I didn't know you were going to be here! Where's Jenna?"

"Um, she's on the couch. When I got here she was on the ground. She hurt her back—tried to pick up too many chairs—so I rescued her, put her on the couch. I'll send you the bill."

Travis' footsteps plod through the living room and he vaults over the couch, landing in front of me. "Honey! Are you okay? Are you in pain?" Travis holds my face in his hands and looks for something in my eyes. He turns back to Collin, then back to me—in his eyes filled with suspicion, and in mine resides guilt. As he cocks his head to kiss me, I turn and offer my cheek. I cannot stand the thought of Collin witnessing Travis' lips locked on mine.

Through the window I watch Travis man the grill, his close friends huddled around him, lobbing Collin the occasional stare of death. There's nothing cute about a grown woman having two men visually dueling over her, but I have to admit, I couldn't ask for a bigger ego boost than this situation, which can only take a nasty turn from here.

As Collin sidles up to the grill with not one, but two plates, Travis plunks down his spatula, his face scrunching up, friends rallying close to his side. He furiously throws his arms up in the air several times, to which Collin shakes his head, his hands thrown up in front of him in an innocent gesture. I watch Travis slam a burger down on each of the plates Collin is holding. *I should go and referee*, I think, but then think better of it: *Even Helen of Troy knew when to bow out of men's affairs.* Collin struts into the living room, and gently draping a napkin across my lap, settles a plate of lunch on my legs.

"Thank you! It's really sweet of you to do this," I purr, watching his eyes angrily dart to Travis who is keeping sentry on us through the window.

"How's your back?"

"It's not hurting, but I don't think I've moved since

you put me here."

"Yeah, that'll help, plus keep taking the ibuprofen. You can have more in a couple of hours. I'll call to remind you."

"Wow! How did you know I love my burger like this—piled high with onions?"

Collin shrugs his shoulders, grinning. "It's how I like my burgers. We must be soul mates, or at least destined to be burger buddies!"

I fiddle with the stack of onions, tucking them neatly back into my sandwich, ready to launch my apology. "I'm really sorry about all of this." The words drip out of my mouth with worry and regret. High maintenance women are rarely attractive for very long, and I don't want him to get the notion that I am not worth the temporary trouble.

"What? You didn't mean to fall or did you? Was that all part of your plan to seduce me?" He laughs.

"No, I mean with Travis. I…I'm not a dishonest person or high maintenance. I am just surprised that you showed up, and by how much I like you. You've swept me off my feet, so to speak." Biting my bottom lip, I offer him my best vulnerable smile.

He clamps onto my leg and laughs, pointing at me. "Yeah! I knew it! You did that on purpose!"

"Oh, I did not!" I reach out and bat at his hair, smoothing it away from his eyes.

A scowl lingers on his face, creasing his forehead. "I think Travis is an asshole; I've always thought that, actually. I don't know why the hell he thinks we're friends. He's just somebody I have to tolerate at work." His eyes shift back over his shoulder as he continues, "What do you see in him?"

"It wasn't necessarily his mind—purely from the waist down. I'm guilty as charged: a horny, sometimes lonely, divorced woman."

"Does he know you feel like that?"

"Well, we haven't really put labels on each other, and neither one of us has required monogamy, so I guess it's a safe assumption to say he does."

"I like your honesty, I really do. It's so much better than playing silly games like a lot of younger women do. You'll be honest with me like that, won't you?"

"Collin, I really don't know any other way to be."

Collin leans over and kisses me on the lips, his sweet wetness lingering there "I'll call you in a couple of days, okay? I'll text you my work number and my email. If you need anything at all, even dirty talk at two in the morning, please call me." He bends over me and finishes his thought, whispering in my ear, "After all of this has blown over and Travis has had a chance to cool off, I promise I'll get you hotter than you've ever been in your life." He crunches me between his arms and seals his words with the best eye fuck I've ever had from him.

He cleans up his plate—and mine—and launches out the door as quietly as possible. The only sound buzzing in my ears is the sound of my heart beating.

I know there is chemistry; I know he has himself together. And I really don't even mind for anyone to know that he's close to having me sprung. What surprises me the most about Collin is how open and vulnerable I make myself with him, and I don't even know him. Could he be someone I might fall in love with? Immediately, I slam the door on that thought. Liking the hell out of him is fine. But love? That simply has to be off of the table; I don't need another heartbreak.

How realistic is it to believe that a woman my age in my situation and a man his age could be anything other than friends with benefits, even if everything in me screams otherwise? Am I just being practical or being practically, impossibly foolish?

Travis stomps across the deck through the back door, a grimace on his face that pulls me kicking and screaming back to reality. I intuit at gut level that I'll have to get rid of Travis at some point very soon—like as soon as the party is over, which may not be soon enough.

This is the boy—the toddler—that is coming out, behavior that I knew I might see at some point, and one of the few downsides to dating younger men.

"So, did rat boy go home?" he demands, jealousy raging in his tone.

"That's not very nice," I respond, using my mother-knows-best tone, demanding, "Why do you call him rat boy?"

"'Cause he looks like a fucking rat!" He narrows his eyes at me, whipping off his ball cap. "Is there something going on between you two? He seems awfully friendly with you, a little too much attention, and a little too touchy-feely with someone else's girlfriend!"

I am certain that my mouth completely unhinges—*Girlfriend? He considers me girlfriend material and I consider him a walking, talking dildo. This is going to be awkward.*

"Travis, I have to be perfectly honest with you. I didn't know you thought of me as your girlfriend. I thought we were just screwing—no strings attached. Remember?"

He scrunches up his face and sits next to me. "I like

you Jenna, and I thought you liked me, but I guess I was wrong." His gaze drops from my face and founders on my hands, which he kneads back and forth between his. "I know I have a lot of growing up to do, and I may not ever be as smart as you'd like for me to be, but I'll always dig you, Jenna—always. Isn't that enough?"

In the background, I hear a television blaring the game, and people shuffling in and out of the kitchen, helping themselves to all I have. When I let Travis help himself to all I had, I assumed he knew my heart wasn't included in the package. In my mind I figured the relationship would run short, sooner rather than later. I simply did not know he was parceling out pieces of himself for the long run. A pang of guilt bolts through me and I reach out for him, tucking his head against my chest, my hand cupping his head. This, also, is one of the downsides to dating younger: spoiling innocence.

"Travis, I'm sorry. I like you, I really do, but I don't see you as ever being anyone I can have a relationship with—the age difference, the pressure from friends, and I don't know, just the fact that you don't really seem to know what you want yet. I believe I do know and I think I want someone who can follow me down that road, even if he's trailing at a snail's pace."

His eyes shift back and forth and his mouth opens, darting out an answer. "Collin is younger than me—he's 26—a couple years younger than me, actually."

"I didn't know that…he seems like he's older."

"But, he's in medical school, and is going to have a real job, an important job, and be a professional soon. That's what you mean, right? That road thing, you want someone who's equal to you, someone who won't embarrass you in front of your friends when you introduce him. Lifeguard and swim instructor at the Kinweld Swim Club is not as impressive as doctor, is it? Dr. Collin…ain't that some shit."

"You've never embarrassed me."

"You've never introduced me to your friends," he reminds me. "I've introduced you to all of mine. And a lot of times someone gives me hell and rags me out, complaining 'Why you wanna go with that old broad? Her tits probably hang down to her knees and her snatch is all dried up!' But, I always defend you, telling them how fine and super smart you are; how you're not like the stupid little twits they run around with and bang; I swear to them that you're absolutely the hottest lay I've ever had, and that it's not just in between your legs, but up here—that's what gets me." He points to his head, then to his heart.

"Fair enough," I whisper, my throat bloated with the proverbial lump.

"I've got plans, you know," he perks up, pacing back and forth in front of me. "You never asked, but I'm going to move up at the club, learn it from the ground up and then swoop in and stun them—when the right position opens, and it's the right time. You should give me another chance, just one, and I promise I won't screw it up—no more weeknight beer pong parties, no more asking you to stay up with me to make prank calls at two in the morning, no more going to the titty bars. I promise I'll do my best to act more like a grown up. I guess it's been a long time coming; I need to act like I'm damn near thirty rather than 13."

All men need mothering, especially the younger ones. They are more vulnerable to life's switchbacks and sharp turns. Travis is practically sitting at my feet now, reminding me of a small child or puppy, desperate for approval, desperate for attention, desperate for whatever he thinks I can offer him. So, I do what comes natural to many women, especially, and unfortunately, for me: I cry.

"Travis," I sniffle, wiping my eyes, "I just don't think it's going to work out between us. I'm sorry. I like Collin too much, and that's not fair to you, especially knowing how you feel about me. But, if you want to carry me upstairs, I'll give you one last chance to love me like…it's the last time. You know I'll miss you, too."

He draws in a breath and laces his fingers together, fidgeting. There is not a hint of a smile on his face. "That's not exactly the answer I had wanted to hear." He pauses, allowing a very faint grin to paint the corners of his mouth. "But, the last part sounds pretty damn good. I'll sure miss hitting that. Rat boy doesn't have a clue what a lucky bastard he is." He swoops down on me, steadying my body in his arms, meandering through the people littered all throughout the house. At my bedroom, he smiles, kisses me, and locks the door behind him.

Very slowly, with deliberate attention, his California-Pacific Ocean-perfect blue eyes never leaving mine, Travis gently draws my t-shirt over my head and pulls my shorts down to my ankles, carefully lifting my legs to remove them. His hands glide over my body, the late afternoon sun throwing shadows across the bed; beads of sweat pop up between my breasts. He lowers his head and laps at them with his tongue. "So sweet," he whispers, moving further down my body, stopping to pull my electric orange panties off.

"Travis?" I say, tapping him on the shoulder. "Um, you don't have to do this. I know this is out of the ordinary—a break-up fuck. Stop if you aren't comfortable."

Wrapping his hands around my wrists, he continues rappelling across my stomach, pinning my thighs down with his shoulders. "Not a chance of that happening," he replies, never being more sure of himself and bravely treading where I'm pretty sure no man has ever tread before, at least in a very long time—brown-eyed Betty.

Gently, his tongue fluffs across my clit and back to my ass; I raise my head, arching my back and watching him watch me getting closer and closer to getting off. His tongue ducks in and out of his mouth, mounting more and more pressure on my clit, the familiar achy wind up beginning inside of me literally the second he sticks his finger in my ass. The wave builds and I extend my legs—taught, my calves resting on his shoulders.

Travis moves one of his hands off of my thigh to circle my ass, clinching it in his palm with every high-pitched-whistling, deep breath I take. I knead the bedspread and never take my eyes away from his until a hundred thousand waves of pleasure unmercilessly break on my body.

"I love eating you…all of you," he groans, crawling up to make his cock meet my mouth. I clench it and stroke his beautiful nine inches, making it come alive, pressing my tongue against the small hole—salty and slightly sticky, coated with his wetness. "Take it all in your mouth. I want to see you gag—with tears."

Opening my mouth as wide as I can, I take a deep breath and devour him, shoving it to the back of my throat. As soon as I get it there, he gives three controlled thrusts, holding the back of my head. My gag reflex overtakes my desire and I try to eject him out of my mouth, but he holds my mouth and head prisoner. Pushing hard against his arms, I suddenly stop, sliding one hand down to my clit, pressing my middle and index fingers hard into it.

Wet and salty, my tears trickle over my nose and down my cheek. Grabbing a handful of my hair, he pulls me back, towering over me, and wiping my tears away with the tip of his dick.

"Did you like that?" Travis asks, but before I have a chance to answer, he commands me to my knees. "I want it doggy style—assume the position." He helps me roll to my knees and plants a firm smack on each butt cheek, followed by a long, wet kiss on each handprint.

"Oh!" I reach back to rub my ass then crane my neck to see that it's pink. "Do I need to give you a safe word?" I joke, slightly concerned that his passion has mixed with his angry streak from earlier.

The demanding glare in his eyes softens. "I'm sorry, babe, want me to stop?"

He is so hot; I know that it has to end with him, especially if I am going to try to move on with Collin, or anyone who can give me more than just a fantastic lay. My eyes drink him up in this vulnerable position—me having the power in the relationship and him playing along as if he is my equal.

Closing my eyes I force this mental image of him into my brain. He looks very much the way he did when I saw him that first time at the pool—innocent, goofy, boyish, charming, and slightly naughty. This is the way I want to remember him.

"No, you don't have to stop, Travis. What do you want me to do? What do you want?"

Unexpectedly, he turns away from me, huddling at

the end of the bed with his arms wrapped around his knees, grabbing at his clothes. "What I want, Jenna, is what I can't have. I think I better leave before one of us gets hurt more."

"Travis, wait, please!" I call from my knees. I hear the door open and close, but from my position, I simply cannot watch him leave. Pulling myself to the head of the bed, I stretch to reach the phone, dialing Fielding.

In between unexpected bursts of tears, I struggle to get my words out to her. "I need you to come over now! I just fuck-broke up with Travis—and I'm stuck in the doggy style position!"

Her cackling response echoes under the thud of my handset hitting the night table.

Chapter Five

Getting What I Deserve—Part I

"Are you better, honey?" Fielding dabs at my eyes and falls helplessly beside me, nearly rolling off the bed in hysterical laughter. "I never, in a billion years, thought that I'd be helping you put your panties on—at least not while we're both sober. Hell! I know you liked the guy, but he's twenty-eight. He's an adult! If he wanted you, and I mean *really* wanted you, he should have piped up sooner about all the girlfriend talk, you know?"

"You're right, but I just feel so guilty! I wish you could have seen his eyes. They were *sooo* sad. It made me feel awful."

"Yeah, you'll miss his dick."

"Fielding! You're terrible!"

"Well, excuse the hell out of me! One of the only things that keeps me going is nasty fantasies about your dalliances! Listen, I know you liked him, and you'll miss him, but remember why you're ending it: Real love trumps really big penises like eighty percent of the time."

"Have you been surfing OMG Sex Facts again?" I ask, ready to stab her in the face with one of the dull crayons my youngest scattered in my bed.

"Don't you like Collin? It's not like you're alone. Geez, I'd love to have two dudes fighting over me."

"Oh yeah, I forgot about that," I coo, remembering

Colin's icy glare and his angry words with Travis.

Mocking me, she jealously adds, "Oh, and yeah, I *forgot* that you didn't just break up with him, you *fuck*-broke up with him. Bitch!"

"Yeah, but he didn't get to come. He called it off after *I* came—poor guy!"

"He did you and didn't get his, too?"

"We didn't exactly have sex—he went down on me, and then to visit Brown Betty."

Fielding clamps down on my arm and gasps. "Wait just a motherfucking minute! You mean to tell me you dumped a fun, gorgeous guy with a giant tool who goes down on you when you break up with him, *and* who gives you an unsolicited rim job *then* lets you selfishly come? Are you insane? I can hardly get my husband to go downtown when we've been married for a thousand years, *and* I had his kids. And a rim job? Forget about that! I'd have better luck asking him to knock off a liquor store. I knew I shouldn't have let him watch the baby squirting out. It ruined it. Travis really did fuck your brains out, didn't he?" She shakes her head, lobbing angry looks at me. "You should be ashamed of yourself! You should have at least jerked him off or something."

"I tried but he left! He just…turned off and left."

"Well, you know I want the best for you, and I want to see you happy. So, I hope Collin is worth it. What will you do if he has a tiny itsy bitsy cock?" She giggles, teasing me by holding up her pinky in my face.

"I guess I'll have to crawl back to Travis," I snort. "I'm glad we're friends, and that you think nothing of racing to my house at dinner time to help me with my man woes, and my panties. But you know what I appreciate most?"

"You appreciate my sarcastic, brutally honest, down-home wit?"

"No, the fact that you don't judge me or what I do, or don't do. I was a good girl when I got married, and now look at me. You've never said you think I'm acting like a whore—a greedy whore."

Fielding hugs me and doesn't let go. Patting me on my back she responds, "Well, what's good for the goose is good for the gander! I'll *never* stoop to calling you a whore because you're simply acting like a woman with a man's morals."

****

At eleven o'clock that night, the phone blares out at me, and I nearly hurt myself reaching for it. I assume it's my ex—one of the kids is sick or he's in a funk and wants to talk.

"Jenna?" Collin's voice jumpstarts my heart; my blood quick-throbs through my veins.

"Yeah, it's me."

"Uh, it's Collin. Your friendly neighborhood medical professional for hot, single women."

"What?" I laugh hysterically, steadying my back. "Hmmm...maybe. The name rings a bell, but I can't quite get the face. Of course I remember you! You're not exactly easy to forget, friend. You know, you're late with your pharmacy reminder. I'll have to report you to the licensing board, unless...you can convince me otherwise."

"Well, we'll have to see what I can do about that. I hope I can meet your expectations."

"I have no doubt that you can, Collin."

"How'd it go with Travis?" The catch in his voice betrays him. He's checking up on me.

"Uh, well, he was upset, but I think he'll be alright. We left things in a decent spot."

"What does that mean?" Jealousy stokes his response.

I sigh and know that this is not going to be a short conversation. Young dudes need to be taken by the hand and told—as well as shown—how things work in very simple terms. Taking a deep breath, I wipe the last image I have of Travis from my mind.

"I was honest with him about my feelings for you and told him I couldn't see him anymore. He was a little sad, but he understands it's over."

"Oh, yeah, that's cool. Are you alright with that?"

"Well, if I wasn't okay with it, I don't think I'd be talking to you right now," I answer, slightly annoyed at his oblivious eleven p.m. phone call.

I can practically hear him smiling through the phone. His next question is breathy and desperate. "When can I come over to take you out?"

"How about we meet for lunch next week? Does Wednesday work for you?"

"Yeah, I get out of class just before one. Is that too late?"

Now it's my turn: Remembering just how young he is, I take a deep gulp and try to concentrate on my words and not on the excitement building between my legs. "Sure. One o'clock would be great. If you tell me where you'll be I'll swing by and pick you up—in front of your dorm or on a street corner. Shit! This makes me feel like such a naughty old biddy."

"You are a naughty old biddy! I hope you don't hurt me."

"If I do, I promise you'll love every second of it.

You might learn a thing or two."

"Yeah, well, I can hold my own. I'm no sixteen-year-old kid who doesn't know what he's doing. I can please a woman, and I can go a long time. *I* might surprise *you*. But, we're getting ahead of ourselves."

I'm aware of my own heavy breathing into the phone and I inhale deeply, resisting the urge to touch myself. *But oh, how I want to touch myself!* If he's as confident in bed as he is everywhere else, he'll definitely surprise me, not to mention spoil me for everyone else in the thirty-and-under category.

"So, where does a naughty girl pick up a hot, young stud on a Wednesday at one?"

"In front of the biological sciences building—just pull into the fire lane and wait for me. If the traffic cops run you off, just circle the block and I'll find you."

"That sounds good, Collin. Thanks for calling, and I'm really looking forward to our date."

"Me too, sweetheart. Don't forget to take your ibuprofen and rest that back for another day or so. Good night, my hot little honey."

I put the phone down on the nightstand and let my mind wander…as well as my fingers. It is killing me not to have him, but I firmly believe the wait will be well worth it. Until then, I'll just have to be happy diddling myself.

Chapter Six

Getting What I Deserve—Part II

"I think you may be the only human with whom I have come into contact who actually knows the whereabouts of the last Pizza Pie Palace on earth. Why'd you pick *this* dump for lunch?" The edges of Fielding's mouth crimp tightly as she tries not to touch the table.

"Aw, I'm trying to save my money. I've got an appointment at Be Beauty Medispa to have my stomach done."

"What the hell is wrong with you? What about our plastic surgery pact? Remember our cheer?" She holds her knuckle pom-poms up in front of her. "Injections are for bitches afraid of the stitches and tummy tucks are for lazy fucks who eat too many dishes. Jenna, don't be a dolt! You don't need plastic surgery."

"It's not surgery. It's a procedure that uses radio frequency to heat up the fat and skin to make it all disappear—naturally—nice and tight." I snap my fingers in the air in front of me. "You know I've never liked my stomach, not even in college, and especially now after the kids."

She stops in the middle of inhaling her garlic breadstick, politely removing it from her mouth. "Look, do whatever you want, but honestly, I think you're pretty freaking awesome, and if young stud doesn't like it, then screw him, that's what I say." Fielding turns toward our prison-bait-aged waiter and deep throats her breadstick, smiling, seductively pinning him a tempting look; she slowly draws it out of her mouth with a trail of spit teasing him. "We'll have a large pepperoni pizza—real pepperoni—no roadkill pepperoni like you hicks around here like to serve—and tell the jail chef that if he screws us on the cheese, I'll call his parole officer."

"What was *that*?" I demand, choking on the cola as it nearly fizzes out of my nose.

"I can look, too, can't I? Cliff went to a strip club the other night with his friends, so I owe him big time." She dwells on the basket of breadsticks a little too long. "I'm not pissed, but I guess I'm feeling insecure. It sucks getting older, doesn't it?"

I surf Fielding's eyes and clench onto a sadness and disappointment that I've not seen before. She's been that unwavering anchor for me for so long that honestly I forgot it's possible that she has issues, too. Her life appears to be so picture perfect from the outside. "If you didn't want him to go, why didn't you let him know how much it bothered you?"

"It's not that I didn't want him to go, it's just that I'm afraid he won't be attracted to me anymore after seeing all the young, luscious babes. Or, maybe I'm just not feeling attractive, or feeling left out because you're back in the game with the young and the irresistibly hot. I don't know. I guess I'm just restless."

"You're still attractive to him, and you know that physical attractiveness is only a small part of any relationship, especially for Cliff the Brain. How could you even think that a college professor, especially *your* college professor—could ever be any other way?"

Exasperated, I chomp the end off of a breadstick, adding, "Don't you remember how he chased you for nearly a year before you'd even give him the time of day? That's love."

"Cliff's co-worker David left his wife of fifteen years for a twenty-two-year-old grad student. It happened last week. Apparently they got chummy over the past year while working together on her thesis about the evolution of women in the porn industry."

"Ouch! I guess that involved some research, so to speak?"

"Yeah, and David's wife, Kelly, found some of that research. The piece of shit recorded a few of their encounters on his iPhone. Go figure. I guess he *wanted* to get caught. Anyway, he told her he was in love with this other woman. She filed for divorce and took the kids to live with her parents."

"You're worried about Cliff now?"

Then, the dam breaks. Fielding has always had a propensity to tear up, but very rarely does she let the waterworks run free, yet today, the flood cometh.

I slide around to her side of the booth and put my arm around her, trying to reassure her. As a woman on the other side of forty—forty-and-a-half to be exact—I have had time to digest what it means to be seen as "old" even though I don't feel that way. One day I noticed that my skin is not as firm as it used to be, the fine lines creeping in around the eyes, the young clerks in the stores who automatically call me "ma'am" and mean it—but I have made great strides in understanding.

I have only just recently discovered why forty is called the new twenty: Because at forty, I may not look quite as good as someone half my age, but I've replaced the collagen with confidence, and you can't buy that—it's a hard-earned quality. I am financially secure and finally happy in my own skin. I'm a hell of a lot happier than I ever was in my 20s. I can look back over my shoulder at the trail that I have left, and be proud of it. I no longer fear losing my way because I've arrived.

Fielding, like a lot of women, is still on the cusp of discovering her purpose, on the precipice of no longer being young, but not exactly old either, and freaking out about it—and a very normal freaking out. As long as society continues to glorify physical youthfulness over experience, and puts beauty at the top of the pecking order, we're all only one bad wrinkle away from insanity.

"Fielding, some people might call this a midlife crisis, but I can tell you, think of this as a midlife chrysalis. You are about to open up and discover some of the best days of your life. I know it sounds like bullshit, but if you can get to the point where I am, to the point of acceptance, to the point of really being proud of who you are and what you've accomplished, to the point of *finally* being comfortable with your body and your sex appeal, you will be okay. Besides, you've got another three months before the big day. Relax and enjoy still being in your thirties."

She doesn't lift her face out of her hands, but continues to shake her head back and forth. I dig in my purse for a tissue and shove it between the holes of her laced fingers. Our prison-bait waiter quietly repositions our drinks and places the pizza on the table stand, delicately cutting it into perfect triangles. Over the rattle of our plates, I watch Fielding's thin body vibrate through her tears, and wonder how I could have ever missed my dearest friend's suffering. I must be evolving into a nympho—an incredibly selfish nympho.

"Is there something else wrong? Something that you want to tell me, but couldn't because I've been too busy being selfish?" I ask.

"Cliff and I have been having problems, nothing big, nothing that I think will ruin us—at least for right now— but sometimes I wonder what it would be like…"

"To be single? To be without your kids, even for just a couple of days? To be like me?"

"Yes, like you."

"That's funny. I am just sitting here thinking how wonderful your life is, Fielding, even with the bumps in the road. Unfortunately, the grass never stops being greener, does it? No matter how hard you keep looking across that fence. And for the record, there's a lot about my life that sucks. Don't think it's champagne and big cocks every weekend, Ms. Baller. A lot of times I'm lonely, and frustrated, and overwhelmed with all the responsibility that I have, that was forced on me— responsibility that I chose. I often wonder what it would be like to be in love with a great guy, a guy who has always been there for you, who's smart and dependable, and who wants to please you. Someone who craves me, the way Cliff craves you. I see it in his eyes, it's on his heart Fielding, he does. I know it."

"That's not what is bothering me. I'm not sure *I* crave him anymore. I'm just not sure whether he's enough. Tell me he is Jenna, tell me he simply has to be."

"Look, I don't think I can tell you how or what to feel. You have to figure that out for yourself if you want to be truly happy. Don't give up on him, Fielding, just give yourself time."

"What if I can't?"

"Well, I'll be here for you no matter what—and you can live in my basement."

She wipes her cheek with the back of her hand and gives our prying waiter a backward glance. With a criminal grin, she asks, "What do you think he's like?"

I size him up and finish her thoughts. "He's inexperienced, but eager to please. Sometimes, those are the best kind."

"We should go out this weekend. I need a break from the kids, and Cliff. There's a new bar opening— The Lizard's Hatch."

"Sounds like a redneck biker bar." I cringe.

"No, it's a new bar—for the college crowd."

"Well, I was going to save this as a surprise for your birthday next week, but since I've got all the details worked out with your awesome husband, whose blessing I have, I'll just tell you now. This Saturday night I'm going to sweep you away to a time, a time from the past when life was less complicated, where debauchery dominated—"

"Just get on with it! Tell me!"

"Wanna go west to Nashville to see the 80s Hunks Concert—Springfield, Adams, and Idol?"

Fielding screams and jumps up in the seat of the booth. "Hell yes! Let's go now!"

I throw a twenty on the table and watch as Fielding plants a giant wet kiss on our waiter's cheek. I may not ever fully recover from this weekend.

Chapter Seven

Pleased to Tease or Why Nothing Can Ever Be Simple

As soon as I walk into the door from work, the kids begin to bicker, and my oldest son sucker punches Jacob—the youngest—for no apparent reason. My daughter cries about an older girl making fun of her nail polish on the playground. My oldest, Bennett, cries about a book report he has to do, but hasn't read the book yet, and he's hungry. The middle child (oh, and isn't it always the middle child?)—daughter—screams because she is frustrated with algebra, and because that is what she does best these days. Of course, *she's* hungry, too. Dinner to fix, laundry to wash and fold, homework to knock out, and I'm the only grown-up here. Welcome to Monday in the life of the single mom. Sometimes, I just want to sit down and cry.

In the middle of my marinara sauce, and another sibling rivalry, the phone rings.

"Hello!" I practically yell into the phone, annoyed that the person calling has no idea how annoying his call is to me right at this moment.

"Ms. Craig? This is Elaine from the Be Beauty Medispa. I'm just calling to confirm your appointment tomorrow—three o'clock, Tuesday afternoon. Remember to wear loose fitting pants, and—"

"Yes, yes, yes! I remember. I'll be there. This is really not a good time, but thank you for the reminder." I hang up and plunge the pasta into the boiling water, yelling at the children to keep their hands to themselves—again—and then the phone rings—again.

"Hell-O!" I growl, ready to jump through the receiver.

"Um, Jenna?"

I melt like butter in a hot pan. It's Collin.

In any relationship there is what I call the great equalizer. For example, a great guy with a big dick, but he *is* a dick; a pretty girl with no personality; an ugly girl with an awesome personality, but no game because no one wants to take a chance with her; and in the May-December department, an attractive single woman who's ready to mingle, but she's got to mingle around her children, and her children's schedules; and a hot, young dude, who's clueless about a single working mother and how he can fit into the mix. In all combinations of people in relationships, there is an equalizer. It's the thing that should, theoretically, keep you honest and on your game. It's the universe's answer to our human ability to muck everything up. So, Collin—delicious, sexy, wonderful Collin— is clueless, and the question is, do I let him continue to be clueless or do I clue him in?

"Hey! Listen, sweetie, I'd love, I mean really, *really* love to chat with you, but could I call you back in a couple of hours, maybe when my kids go to bed? They're circling me like piranha, and I'm scared, very scared…Must. Get. Dinner. Ready." I giggle, thinking that I've gently clued him in to an important time and role in my life: dinner time with Chef MILF. But, his answer is silence, followed by a long, tortured sigh.

"Oh, well, I was going to take you out to dinner, but…"

I wanted this to be as painless and honest for him as possible. "But, you kinda forgot about the kids?"

"It's not that, but, well, yeah, I'm a single guy. I just eat whenever my schedule allows me to. That's me; that's how the life of a future doctor rolls."

"Yeah." I laugh, not sure I'm relieved, or how well I'm playing this. "I remember those days, and I look forward to them every weekend when the kids are gone. You know, I've got plenty for dinner—wanna come over? Just keep in mind it is spaghetti night; it won't be pretty. I have a four-year-old. You might want to wear something dark—like a two-ply garbage bag."

I know I've charmed him when I hear him crack up—the belly-busting kind. "I'd love to. I love spaghetti. And you know what else I love, you wonderful, interesting woman I can't wait to see?"

My heart flutters in my throat and I'm hardly able to utter the words, "No, what?"

"I love your honesty and your sense of humor. You are wittier than hell. I'll be there in about fifteen minutes. Could I bring some wine and maybe some dessert?"

"Absolutely, that'd be great! See you in a few."

If I were butter in a hot pan, I'd be scorched. *Yeow! What a man!* I scream to myself. Quickly, I snatch up the phone and punch Fielding's number.

She answers with "If you're calling to tell me he has a huge penis, I'll cut it off and beat you with it."

"No! He just called to take me out, but kinda forgot about the kids. Well, long-story-short, he's coming over—it's spaghetti night." Putting my hand over my heart, I calmly breathe through my nose, taking deep breaths.

"Damn girl. This guy must dig you. I mean he's really into you. Either that or he's stupid. Did you tell him it was spaghetti night? Did you tell him you have a small child *and* it's spaghetti night?"

"Yeah. I called the kids piranha and told him to wear a garbage bag."

"You better get laid tonight." The line goes dead and my cheeks ache from smiling so much.

I scamper to set another place at the table, and while in super-lightning-fast-Mario mode, lecture the kids. *Mommy is having a new friend over, so let's mind our manners—no fighting, yelling, screaming, or throwing anything, okay?*

Our dinner is perfect—picture perfect in fact—so much so that I am driven to question Stephen Hawking's theory on parallel universes. I must be in one because no one farts or belches at dinner, no one talks about poop or puke, no one is sassy or rude, and everyone chews with his or her mouth closed, for the most part. *This must be a freaking fantasy—one that I hope I never leave.* Collin even helps with the dishes, skulking over and standing very close behind me, grinding into my backside.

"You like that?" His hot moist breath hangs heavy in my ear; his hands trace my ribs and cup my breasts, finding my nipples.

I nod, but can hardly speak.

"After we finish with the kids and they go to bed, can I see what kind of sexy lingerie you have on under those work clothes?"

What gets me going the most, what puts the hot in white hot for me is not the sexy talk and breathing, or the hand games, but the "we" of his sentence. "After *we* finish with the kids," as in *him and me*. In the life of a single mother, this is equivalent to offering to go down on her every day without requiring reciprocation, while shaving her legs and picking up her dry cleaning. And, Mr. Take Control delivers. He helps my daughter understand her algebra better than any of her teachers, plays Mad Libs with Bennett, and rules a game of bedtime rock-paper-scissors with Jacob.

As the house quietly settles down, we snuggle on the couch with our wine.

"So, you couldn't wait until Wednesday for your naughty rendezvous with me?"

"Nope. I could not. I also wanted to let you know that my roommate will be out all of Wednesday afternoon, if you really want to kick it old school." His eyebrows dart up and down on his face, letting me know that his brand of kink is right up my, well, you know…

"Mmmm…that sounds absolutely yummy. I think I might be sick Wednesday afternoon."

"I hope so." Collin takes our wine glasses to the kitchen and on his way back over to me he begins unbuttoning his shirt, having it completely undone by the time he is standing over me. Reaching up, I sweep my hands across his chest and let the shirt fall back over his shoulders; I go in for his glasses next.

"I don't want your beautiful, blue eyes hiding behind those glasses."

The corners of his mouth turn up and his eyes dart down to the floor. "You like the way I look without my glasses?"

"I like the way you look—period. You are so sexy! It makes me hot." I kiss his guns—muscular, smooth skin, flexing, sprinkled with a fine layer of sweat. I continue to let my fingers explore the length of his chest, stopping at his heart to gaze up at him.

"Come here," he whispers.

Collin reaches for my chin and pulls my mouth to his. He allows his lips to linger on mine, clingy from our wetness, slowly devouring me with purpose and intent. He knows exactly how to turn me on. Gently, he tugs at my lower lip, carefully chewing it between his teeth.

Suddenly he detours to my ear lobe and does the same, then the spot behind my ear—*the* spot. I dig my fingers deeper into his guns and an unexpected moan pops out of my mouth from between my wet, soft lips.

He unbuttons my blouse and strings a parade of kisses from my jugular to between my breasts, nibbling on the lacy edge of my bra.

"So beautiful. It makes my mouth water, and makes me want to come all over your rock hard nipples."

Pushing into me, he squirms his way in between my legs, pushing my skirt up to my waist, and thrusts into me again and again; I grind into him, too, the blood pounding. My mound swells and my clit is beginning to ache for satisfaction. Collin moves back to my mouth and gently drives his tongue into my mine, thrusting deeper and harder, moving his hands up to squeeze my tits.

"This feels so good!" he moans. "Just like I knew it would."

"You want to go upstairs?" I whisper in his ear, intending it to be taken as a command, not a suggestion.

He stops kissing me and takes my cheeks in between his palms, exhaling heavily. "I know this is going to sound weird, and I don't want you to think that I'm a tease, but I like to take it slow. I don't just want you to be my sex toy. I like to build up to the main event because I want to be completely comfortable with you, and for you to be completely comfortable with me. Sex is better...*everything* is better that way. What do you think?"

"I think you have amazing wisdom and self-control for a twenty-six-year-old guy, and I think you probably also masturbate a lot. That's something else we have in common."

He laughs and rolls off of me. "Yeah, but it's all about honing one's craft."

"You're smart, you know that?" I ask, nibbling on his fingers.

"I want to make you come on Wednesday," he announces, his smoldering eyes intently staring into mine. "I'll wait to come, but I want to give you that pleasure."

"Oh, Collin. I don't think anyone has ever said that to me, or at least not said it and really meant it." I gulp and he traces my throat with his finger.

"Listen, you need to get to bed. I know you've got work tomorrow, and your kids probably get up early. I did when I was a kid; drove my mom nuts—she's a night owl."

I wrap his shirt back around him and thread the buttons through the holes. "I'm really glad you called, and came by. A lot of guys, especially young ones, are scared of single moms, and especially scared of their kids."

"Well, you might miss out on something great if you exclude that group. Children aren't deal breakers for me. My residency next year is going to be in pediatrics, and I really like kids. Besides, yours are nice. I like being here; it feels cozy."

"See, there you go again with that smart thing," I lecture, poking my finger at his brain. "Keep that up and I'll have to drop to my knees to show my appreciation."

"Oh, and you will, darling, when the time is right. But until then, keep that thing hot for me. I'll see you on Wednesday, and tonight in my fantasy when I jerk off." He seals his tease with a devil-may-care grin.

I linger at the door after our kiss, watching his shadow prowl across the driveway and slither into his car. *How did he get to be so smooth, confident, generous, kind, smart, and sexy as hell? Is he hiding something?* Dating pitfall number two with a young man: It's all too easy to become jaded when it comes to the young. I fall into bed and frig myself to sleep, dreaming of the real thing on Wednesday.

Chapter Eight

Super Momma (AKA Super MILF) Versus the Laser

"Guess what I'm doing right now?" Fielding offers this greeting before I can even hinge open my yap to say hello. She whispers, "I'm looking at dildos—giant, fat dildos. I'm overwhelmed! Which one do I choose? I mean, my first instinct is to go for the porn star model, but I just know that it very well could give Cliff a complex. So, maybe I want something a little smaller, but then again, maybe I should buy two—one public and one private, though I hate to seem greedy."

"Honey," I counter, "you're overthinking this. It's a dildo. There's only one question you need to ask yourself, if you're only going to buy one: Am I going for length or am I going for width? Personally, I'll take a chode any day of the week. Buy two if the mood strikes you, and I'll keep your private *T.rex* dildo here if you want."

"Oooh! Are you offering to make me a sex cave in your basement? I'll have to give you an updated version of my bucket list of RILFs so that you can plaster the walls with old posters."

"What's a RILF?"

"Rockers I'd Like to Fuck, of course! How could you forget that? I'm so stoked for our trip to Nashville!"

"Pace yourself my little sex kitten; we've still got

four days left in the week. Can you still come tomorrow to watch the kids while I have my procedure?"

"Ugh! You're actually going to go through with it?"

"Yeah, of course I am. Everything I've read leads me to believe it's relatively safe, and besides, I've hated my stomach for so long I feel the need to make nice with it again."

"Anything for you, darling—anything. I'll be waiting for them when they jump off the bus. Say, when is your naughty campus rendezvous with Collin?"

"Wednesday at one o'clock! Oh, hell, I get so hot thinking about it! What kind of lingerie should I wear?"

"None—and wear that sexy red suit. When he unwraps you, he'll get an instant boner. It will be the boner to end all boners!"

"Okay, I've got to go before I lose myself to masturbation all afternoon. If you have a chance, swing by to show me your new toy."

"Don't worry, I will! I'm off—to get off."

****

"I'm so glad you picked Be Beauty Medispa, Mrs. Craig. Okay, now before we begin Mrs. Craig—"

"Oh, it's Ms. I'm divorced."

"Well, Ms. Craig, as I told you at your initial consultation, we won't be using any numbing cream because I'll need your feedback to know how hot and uncomfortable the transponder is on your belly. So, while you should not have a lot of pain, I'll warn you that most patients have significant discomfort at some point during the procedure. But, it's short-lived. Once I get the temperature of the skin to 40 degrees Celsius I can start reducing the temperature."

For many women, vanity has no price and no

threshold for which pain is a deterrent. Having birthed three children via c-section (along with three terrible bouts of morning *and* evening sickness during pregnancy) I have grown accustomed to pain. However, I certainly won't say that I have been looking forward to the procedure. "What exactly do you mean by significant discomfort?"

"Oh, you might fidget or yelp. I did have one woman hyperventilate last week."

"I see…" I slowly change into the paper gown and unroll myself onto the table, suspiciously glaring at the machine to my left, trying to look on the bright side, thinking of how tight and luscious my stomach will look after I finish the treatments—all six of them.

The technician squirts some warm gel across my belly; I can't help but think of Collin and smile. *A dirty fantasy couldn't hurt to take my mind off of the pain, right? Maybe I'll just settle in and plan out my moves for tomorrow.*

"Here we go, Ms. Craig. You're on your way to a brand new you!" she eagerly exclaims—a bit too eagerly in my opinion. "Just let me know when you reach the point when the heat becomes unbearable, if you do reach that point."

"Oh, I will," I assure her, beginning my sexy fantasy. I imagine that Collin and I are sitting on his bed in his dorm room; it's quiet, everyone is gone for afternoon classes. It smells like dirty, semen-soaked, sweaty underwear and leftover Ramen noodles. *I hope I don't leave a wet spot on the paper gown!*

"How's the temperature Ms. Craig?"

"Oh, it's heating up nicely," I purr.

I imagine that he peels my ruffled red suit off of me,

my smooth, tanned skin pulsing under his touch. As I pull his face to mine, I look down and see his gigantic cock harden under his soft gym shorts. I reach for it, massaging it until he slides on top of me and pushes his shorts to his ankles. I wrap my heeled feet around his back and gently guide him into me. As he enters, I have to concentrate on breathing—in and out, in and out, again and again—he's almost more than I can handle. But once he's in, he's fabulous, caressing my face and lips with his hands, and his lips, remembering the spot behind my ear. He has perfect control and the perfect stroke—not too deep, not too fast, or too slow, but enough to build up to G spot glory. Just as I drape my legs over his shoulders for the pounding of my life, pain, a very substantial pain, invades my fantasy.

"Oh! Son-of-a-gun that hurts!"

"It hurts so good!" the technician growls as she fiddles with the controls on the machine.

"Yeah, you could say that again," I moan, aggravated by my own vanity.

"Okay, we're all done. I'll need to see you back in a week. You can expect some soreness, tenderness, and redness much like a sunburn. You may use aloe vera gel for topical relief and ibuprofen as needed. Be sure to drink lots of water and do some sort of physical activity. We want to stimulate your lymphatic system to get rid of all that fat. If you have any substantial pain, please let our office know."

Flat on my back, I stare, motionless, at the ceiling for several minutes, thoughts of Collin revolving in my brain. I pull my clothes on with this hope: *Reality has to be as good as my fantasy.*

Opening the door to my house, I hear the happy

sounds of the children, and the smell of the meatloaf I left for Fielding to cook. Not much of a cook, she will gladly act as my supportive partner for a fee—dinner.

"Hey! Super Momma is home. How are you feeling, Super Momma? Let me see that supermodel belly." Fielding rips up my shirt and shrinks in horror. "What the hell did they do to you? It looks like a can of chopped ham down there. Have you looked at this?"

"No. I'm afraid—very afraid. It feels worse than a sunburn—a terrible sunburn. It hurts!" I whine.

"Yeah, like the sunburns we gave ourselves when we were stupid teenagers." Fielding rolls her eyes.

"I'm supposed to drink lots of water and go for a walk, but I don't know how I'm going to do that today. I'm going to feel like such a putz if I have to cancel my date with Collin."

"You can't do that! I need some new masturbation material. Just let me worry with dinner and you go lie down for a while. I'll bring you some ice packs."

I drag myself to my bedroom, half sorry I let my stomach-hating get the best of me. It looks like a sausage—pink, raw, and puckered. A faint knock rescues me from worry.

"Yoo-hoo! I come bearing some relief."

Fielding gently covers me with ice packs, a wicked grin pasted on her face. "Do you want to see my new toy?"

"Oh, yes! Show me, show me!" I clap.

"It's a little unorthodox, but…well, what the hell! I'll just show you.

Looking over her shoulder for sneaking, errant children, she pulls her purse out from under my bed and settles her new friend on her lap.

"Fielding! You are a fucking freak!" I gasp.

"You like it?"

"Uh, well, it's not exactly my style, but that doesn't matter. It's so *big*, and so *black*, and so *studded*. Wow! How is it?"

"Don't know. I haven't had a chance. I was hoping to use it while dinner is cooking, but…well, I can wait until I get home."

"Oh, no, no, no! Please, I couldn't live with myself if I cock-blocked your dildo get-to-know-me time. Have at it. I'll be out here, suffering."

Fielding squeezes me until I yelp and closes the door. She's got the biggest smile on her face that I've seen all week. I think I might hear her own yelp over my meatloaf and mashed potatoes.

Chapter Nine

School Daze

The dratted clock moves more slowly than cold pancake syrup on Wednesday morning. Every conversation, every meeting reminds me of all the driest of business trainings when all you want to do is go to the free happy hour in the hotel lobby. My boss's secretary, a shrew of a brunette named Candy, stops me in the hall. "Are you okay? You look out of it, like you don't feel well."

"Well, actually," I confess, feigning a fever, "I feel a bit flushed. I think there's still flu going around, especially in the schools."

She turns up the collar on her blouse. "Ugh! Have all those kids of yours been sick?"

"No, but sometimes I have to touch their backpacks, and go into the school." I cough into my elbow, trying to hide my dopey smile outlined with secret satisfaction.

She slams the pile of file folders down on her desk. "Well, maybe you should just go home. I hate being sick. It's the considerate thing to do, you know."

I cough again, clutching at my chest. "I know, Candy, I know, but I just have so much to do before these presentations—copies to make, clients to contact."

She motions for me to put my papers on the floor and steps behind her desk, producing a can of disinfectant spray. She douses the papers. "Boss man is out for the afternoon; I can cover for you. I'll make sure the copies and the clients are taken care of." She shoos me out the door. "Go! I mean it! Get out!"

I stop at The Crazy Chicken for a chicken wrap and think, *What a serendipitous situation! No kids, no babysitter issues, no work junk hanging over my head, and the opportunity to get hot and naked with a guy I totally dig. What could possibly ruin this?*

Well before one o'clock, I can't stop my Honda from nervously rolling into the fire lane. I watch over my shoulder, watching for the UT Kinweld campus cops, ready to strike at anything that could ruin my soon-to-be sexy time. At seven after one, Collin rips open the door, gasping for breath.

"Hey!" He slings his backpack on the floorboard. He looks like such a kid—like such a hot, *sexy* kid who is going to screw my brains out.

Leaning across the gearshift, I give him a kiss. "Can I give you a ride little boy? Where are you going? Want some candy?"

His hands dive up under my skirt. "Oooh! I would like a piece of this candy. Goodness, you dirty woman, you're all wet. Did you get all wet waiting for me?"

The only answer I give is this: "You drive, and I'll sit back and enjoy your fingers."

He commands the gearshift with a manly confidence, all the while tickling my legs and giving me the sexiest, most promising looks we've ever exchanged with each other. If he has any idea how hot he is making me, he doesn't let on, which makes me want him even more.

The dorms haven't changed a bit in twenty years,

which puts me in an all young-and-college-horny mood. Collin hooks me around the waist, guiding me past the desk attendant, giving him the secret I'm-about-to-get-lucky head bob. I watch his hands shake as he unlocks the door. The anticipation is killing both of us. By now, I'm so wet that my juice is literally running down my legs.

"My bed is that one—the one on the left."

I turn back around to face him and he's on me, in my face, breathing heavy, pressing into me, smelling me, taking my hair into his greedy hands, pulling me to his mouth and wanting to dominate me.

"The smell of perfume on your skin is so beautiful it makes me want to explode. I don't think I could physically let you go right now, even if I had to," he murmurs.

Our lips crash and we desperately draw breaths between kisses; he roughly works the buttons through the holes of my jacket and then my skirt. Taking Fielding's advice, the only thing I am wearing under my suit is my perfumed body lotion.

Collin draws in a noisy breath and lets it slowly escape between his lips, blowing across my nipples and drawing down to my stomach, which he caresses and kisses. On weak knees, I sink to the bed, opening my legs to make room for him. He's tall—very tall—and even on his knees we're almost at eye level. I pull his t-shirt over his head and see he's sweating—excited, nervous, anticipating our first encounter. When I get to his shorts, he helps with the button, nearly popping it off, as tight as it is with his very visible hard-on.

This is it! I tell myself. *This is the big reveal. Don't be disappointed if he's not like Travis. There's more to a boyfriend than a big cock.*

As soon as I wrap my hand around him, he sighs in relief, and I do too; he's not as long as Travis, but every bit as thick. My favorite: a chode. And he's as stiff as he could possibly be.

"I don't think I've ever held such a hard cock," I moan, feeling the blood course through it.

"You make me so hot. This is perfect, you are perfect—me and you, skin on skin—I knew you'd look good *on* me, but not as good as I'm going to look *in* you."

Throwing my head back, he moves down to suck my nipples while I stroke him, gently squeezing his balls. "Collin, I know you said that you wanted to wait, but I don't think I can. If I don't have you, I'm going to explode into a thousand little pieces," I confess, hotter than a whore at a Las Vegas convention.

He goes lower still, lingering between my legs, licking my thighs, touching his hot lips all along my crotch.

I bring my mouth to his and taste my sweet juice on his tongue, motioning him to take my seat on the bed. On my knees, I estimate that his cock might be a good inch shorter than Travis', but as I begin to suck it, I practically have to unhinge my jaw to get the beast in my mouth. This man is exactly what I like—EXACTLY.

Smiling up at him, my tongue seals his entire shaft in sticky saliva, trailing from my mouth to the tip. I force his cock as far back into my mouth as possible and rhythmically jerk him—my lips, my tongue sliding up and down, my left hand squeezing his balls while he bucks and moans. Opening my eyes to watch him watching me, he is pinching the bridge of his nose with his fingers and squinting.

"What's wrong?" I ask, stopping.

"Nothing! Not a damn thing! I'm just trying to keep from coming."

Ladies, if you've been there, or even if you haven't, you know there is no nicer compliment than premature ejaculation—even if it only *almost* happens, and even if it temporarily sets back your mojo, it's nice to know you've still got *it*.

I come up for air and climb to straddle him, my ass hanging off of his lap, and he helps himself to a handful of it, sliding me sideways to the bed. I open my purse and pull out a condom.

He shakes his head. "Nah, those regular condoms don't fit so well. I gotta have something a little roomier. like these." He holds up an extra large condom.

No sweeter (or truer!) words could have been spoken. I greedily watch as he readies himself and gently climbs on top of me. We grind and kiss, and he remembers the spot behind my neck, lingering there while I feel the tip of his cock getting closer and closer to putting out my fire.

As he thrusts, I grab my legs and pull them up, holding them at my sides, nearly ready to explode myself. Just another two pumps and he'll be all the way inside me, and I'll be on the other side of our universe— the creamy, milky way.

Then, reality rears its ugly mug. If you fake something bad happening in order to get something good to happen, the universe will seek to right itself, and quite possibly, to pay you back for your smug impudence in believing you could actually manipulate your reality.

On the verge of my first phenomenal, awesome orgasm with Collin, the lock on the door rattles open and the bathroom door frantically seals tight. A series of machine gun rapid-fire farting noises are the only sounds we hear—at first—then moaning. Collin stops and pulls a sheet over us, yelling, "Hey! Mason! What the hell are you doing here? I thought you had class all afternoon—and a lab. What the *hell*? I told you I had something special going on, remember? I need you to be gone!"

"Uh! Yeah, sorry! I got the shits man—bad! I ate at The Crazy Chicken today at lunch—bad move, dude, bad move." More distressed bowel noises emanate from behind the bathroom door, which are not especially conducive to orgasms—his or mine.

Collin swipes his brow and laughs, rolling off of me. "I am so, *so* sorry. He's an idiot."

My mind keeps swirling around his roommate's words: The Crazy Chicken, lunch, the shits. I tell Collin, "Ask him *when* he had lunch today," I curiously inquire, wondering whether I could be next, and how long I had to keep my decency.

"Why?" he asks, befuddled.

"Uh, because I had lunch there today, too—about an hour ago."

"Hey! Mason! When did you eat there today man—know the time?"

"Yeah, right when they opened—eleven in the morning. Damn! I'll never eat there again."

"When did you eat there?" Collin asks, pointing at me.

"Between noon and 12:30—right before I picked you up. I guess I better head home; it looks like I could only have an hour before the fun begins."

"Oh, and leave all of this?" Collin laughs, but pinning a distressed look on his face. "Is this a bad sign?

Does this put you off?"

"No! Of course not! It's not your fault. Next time, though, and believe you me, there will be a next time very, very soon, we'll have fun at my house. I'm going out of town with my friend Fielding this weekend, but I'm not doing anything this Friday, and the kids will be with their Dad. Are you still interested?" I purr, nibbling on one of his sexy, tight guns.

"I can't on Friday, I mean, I could, but…well…I have swim practice, and after it's over, I'm usually pretty beat. Usually, I grab a bite to eat and go home—straight to bed. I don't think I'd be much in the sack. Can we do it tomorrow?" he asks hopefully.

"Oh, honey, I'd love to, but my daughter has a dance recital at seven, and tomorrow is a long day at work, too. I usually take off early on Fridays to meet my ex and do the kid swap thing. What kind of swim practice do you have?"

"I'm practicing for the World Swim Competition trials. I swam in high school, got a sweet scholarship for school, and managed to qualify for the trials. I'm super stoked about it, too! Last time around, I just missed qualifying for the World Swim Competition in London, so I can't let up. I'm sorry sweetheart."

"Are you kidding me? Don't be sorry at all. That's one of the coolest things I've heard in a long time! You—the World Swim Competition. Wow! You're smart, hot, nice, *and* a star athlete. What other talents are you hiding?"

"Well, if the shitting idiot hadn't barged in, I could have shown you. Would it be terrible to wait until the weekend after next? I don't want to be interrupted. *And* I don't want to be rushed. I just want you all to myself.

Can we have a sleepover at your place?" His baby blue eyes wrap me in the promise of the sweetest, hottest boning I've surely ever had—at least in a couple of months. He watches me get dressed—suit and shoes, and shakes his head with several gulps interjected in between his roommate's indecent bowel noises.

"You are fine. You are one sexy, classy lady, you know that? I am *so* sorry about today, but I promise, next time…" he reaches out and pinches my ass.

"Next time I'm gonna rock your world," I finish his thought and we stand outside in the hall kissing for fifteen minutes, lingering, pulling away, only to dive right back in again.

Friday morning, I wake with Collin's scent still lingering on me—and in me. I don't want to wash his smell off, so I grab my dildo, Big Blue, and lay back, ready to replay my Wednesday memories—minus the roommate sound effects—and frig myself silly before the kids wake up.

Suddenly, my personal porno is interrupted by a brilliant idea: I will whip up a surprise gourmet picnic for Collin after swim practice tonight. He may not be in the mood for more than eating and cuddling, but at least a girl can try.

Normally, surprises (good surprises) can be a beneficial, if not a tricky way to get to the guts of any relationship. I still can't shake the feeling that Collin is hiding something—or someone—despite the fact that he is willing to wait for perfection. I figure he's either really into me and really does want to make it awesome, is unsure of himself, or has something else he's hitting on the side; or, any combination of the above. *Who says relationships get any easier as you get older?* The problems with them don't necessarily change a lot, but the solutions quickly become much clearer. Sooner or later, it's a matter of learning when to trust your instinct.

I bow out of Friday lunch with Fielding and rush to The Goode Market—olives, cheese, crackers, fried chicken fingers, and a cold salad round out my playbook. I pack one beer, just for the two of us. I think he'll need to be relaxed for what I have planned.

Outfitted in my sleeveless sundress and wedge sandals, I strut into the swimming complex across from Collin's dorm. Save the occasional coaching voice, the pool area is relatively quiet, except for the sound of water being paddled and pushed under the swimmers. It's nearly 8:45 p.m. and practice will be ending soon.

I'm hypnotized watching the relays. He is a beautiful, powerful swimmer, his great guns and long strong legs propelling his body through the water like a dolphin. He is strong and lean, his muscles taught from the constant intense workout.

From the safety of the upper deck of bleachers, I lust after him—the star in a naughty peep show of young college athletes. I resist the urge to wave, or even move, waiting for him to discover me. I stare at him, drinking up his fine toned, wet body thrusting across the endless length of the pool. I gather the full skirt of my strapless sundress between my legs and slide my pink bikini bottom far to the side with a naughty laugh. I spread my legs open, hoping he might see—everything. Suddenly, Collin stretches his neck and shields his eyes from the pool floodlights, staring high into the darkened bleachers. We smile at exactly the same time.

"Hey! I see you up there, spying on me. I'm coming up there to get you!" Collin hoists himself out of the deep end of the pool and takes the steps—two at a time—until he reaches me. His abs are ripped, tight, and tempting. I have to remember we have an audience. In his swim shorts the outline of his package is almost more than I can bear and I bite my lip to remind me to stop staring. I pick up the picnic basket and let my fingers brush against him and linger. A wave of ecstasy washes across his face.

"What do you have there?" he whispers with a sideways glance, reaching down to adjust himself.

"I brought a picnic. I wanted to see you. Wednesday was just jungle hot, and I knew I absolutely could not wait to see you again, to touch you again, to taste you."

His lips part in a sexy smile, amazed at his luck. "Wow! I don't know what to say. This is a first."

"Is there someplace where we can go?"

Before he can answer, a brunette sidles up behind him, playfully pinching at his sides. "You going out with us?" she demands, snubbing her nose at me. She is territorial and guarding the space she shares with him, her knee jutted between my body and Collin's.

"Uh, no, not tonight. I've got other plans. Tell the guys maybe next week, or wait…" he grins my way, remembering our plans. "Probably not next week either. I've got other plans."

"Oh," she answers, deflated.

I extend my hand to her. "Hi, I'm Jenna Craig."

"I'm Samantha—Samantha Jordan." Her shake is weak and clammy.

Collin smacks himself in between the eyes. "I'm sorry ladies, I spaced out! Samantha, Jenna is…" he lingers over his words, "my new girlfriend."

"Hmmm. Well, I'm his coach, and *ex*-girlfriend." She punctuates her words with laser focus on the ex.

Clearly, she's not over him, and with good reason. History between people is important, and in many relationships, keeps couples together, especially if that history includes children. But, unfortunately, Samantha has yet to learn that history usually means nothing in the case of twenty-something growing pains. He is growing up into the man he wants to be, and growing apart from her.

Collin swipes his hand down his face. He is in an awkward position and rattles on about how he and Samantha coached the Kinweld High School swim team together for several seasons, and about how she helps coach everyone on the team—with an emphasis on the everyone. However, it's not enough to break her death stare on me, so I decide to try and kill her with kindness.

"Well, Collin and I were just about to have a picnic. There's plenty here if you'd like to join us. I'd love to hear more about how the prospects for the World Swim trials are shaping up."

"No thank you," she passes icily. "I've got to be heading out." She tromps down the steps in defeat.

Several minutes pass before Collin says anything, instead awkwardly wringing his shoulders with his hands. "Sorry about that. It's still kind of weird, you know, being around the ex. I guess I should have told you, but...well, we really hadn't gotten there yet."

"I understand. It's okay. I have an ex, too, you know, and I have to see him every week, but it doesn't mean that I'm into him, even though I still do care about him."

I watch a light bulb go off in his head. "Yeah, that's exactly how I feel. I want her to be happy, but we just can't be happy together anymore. It's been hard on her, though, trying to put distance between us when we have to see each other every week."

"It gets easier, just give it time." I pat his tush.

"You are so easy to be with Jenna. I think that's why I like you so much." He reaches over and pushes the hair off of my neck, kissing it then moving to my mouth. "I am so glad you came by this evening. I had wanted to get this off of my chest for the last week."

"I'd like to get something off of my chest, too—this dress. Think you can help me with that?"

"I sure can, but think we can eat first? I'm starving!" He snorts, wrapping me against the hard wetness in his suit. "That was really nice, what you offered to Samantha. Did you really mean it?"

"Well, of course. We're all grown-ups here, aren't we?"

Thank goodness for ulterior motives—and for the darkness of the bleachers.

We perch high in our loft, discussing the trials and the kids, and anything else that pops into our minds, including my unfortunate Crazy Chicken dining disaster and its aftermath. It truly is easy being with him, too. For the first time since my divorce, I think, *Here's someone who might actually deserve the love I want to give, albeit with a lot of trepidation.*

"Want to go down to the locker rooms?" He nudges me.

"I guess so. We won't get in trouble will we?"

"Nah! I know the guard. He won't even notice."

We launch down the steps, stopping for a detour at the edge of the pool. I peel my clothes off, a hot pink bikini underneath, and I jump in. He follows me, whisking me up tightly in his arms, staring at me.

"You are so beautiful. I think you may be the most

beautiful woman I've ever seen, the most beautiful woman I've *almost* had."

"Are you too tired?"

"I'm too tired to make love to you the way I want to, Jenna. I really, *really* want it to be special for us—the whole deal."

"Well, then, how about a blow job?"

He curiously tilts his head, looking around us. "Let's move to the whirlpool room. There's a wall to hide us from the cameras. "You don't mind?"

"If I did, I wouldn't be offering."

He sits on the side of the whirlpool and I pull his swim shorts to his knees and off. I lick the tip of his cock and plant wet kisses all down the shaft, until I get to his balls, which I put in my mouth and gently suck, fingering that spot between his balls and his ass that he probably doesn't even know he likes, but right now he does. He moans—a profanity-laced love train of compliments.

Moving back to his cock, I watch him, watching me licking my lips and juicing up his shaft, ready to inhale his awesome. There's not a lot of frills with this blow job—I'm stroking it, deep-throating it, and working my tongue along the shaft until I think I've nearly sprained it, but it's worth it.

"Oh, Jenna! Don't stop baby. Please don't stop. I want to come in your mouth. Will you show me? Show it to me!" he hisses, ready to drop his load.

I am reenergized and take it deeper down my throat, squeezing it harder, moaning and writhing on his leg, my other hand pressing hard into my clit. His chest fans out and his stomach dips as he gets closer. His legs are wound tightly around my back. I come, and at the same time jack fiercely on his fat cock as he explodes in my mouth. I open to let him see—his cum dripping down my chin onto my tits, where I rub it into my nipples, giving him a lingering gaze of wanting more.

"That was amazing. You could win an award for that."

"Is there one for blow jobs?" I ask, fishing for another compliment.

"If there was, you'd win gold. I don't think they'll put your picture on a box of cereal for that, though—but they should!" he grins, totally satisfied.

"I can't wait to see *your* hot ass on a box of cereal! Actually, I think I might want to see a different body part on there, but they'd have to cover the whole box with brown craft paper like dirty magazines in the mail." I laugh and he kisses me, and we giggle, lingering by the pool, French kissing and nervously looking over our shoulders. From the corner of my eye, I see Samantha's blue and green jacket darting out the door.

Chapter Ten

Hoochie Momma

Saturday morning I pick up Fielding at her house. I wish I could say I am as excited as she is, but the awkwardness of seeing Collin's ex-girlfriend at his practice is really digging at me. I tell myself, *She's not a direct threat, but any contact with an ex is contact that could be poison to a new relationship. I've got to take it to the next level with Collin. And fast.*

"Nashville! Nashvegas! The last time we were in Nashville we saw your cousin Gary doing a drag show as Pam Cochran. Remember that? He was a dead ringer for her!"

"Hmm, yeah, I do remember. He was lovely, especially the gown—canary yellow I believe," I reply, unaware of Fielding's glare on me.

"No! No, no, no! You're not going to be someplace else in your head while I'm here. I *know* that look! Spit it out. That's what girlfriend weekends are for."

"Well, I saw Collin last night."

She reaches over and slams the radio button, switching it off, and crosses herself. "Please, tell me he's hung like a horse."

"I didn't know you were still Catholic. I thought you switched."

"Eh, I did, but it didn't take, so I decided to switch

back. Anyway, tell me. Is it what I said? Oh, honey, I'm so sorry! He's got a smidgen of a member?"

"No! He's got a nice one—a chode—fat but not too long. It's just what I like."

"Oooh! So, did it happen last night?"

"No, he had swim practice—with his ex-girlfriend. And, that's the problem. He says he's not interested in being with her, but with her around all the time…"

"Jenna, are you jealous? *You*? I haven't seen this side of you, well, since your very mature news reporter fling kissed your hand with his smirking girlfriend waiting right behind him. Okay, let's think about this logically. Who's substantially hotter, really?"

"Uh, I am. In fact, he said he broke up with her for me, basically."

"Okay, what does his wing-a-ding say?"

"It didn't say anything; it just stood at attention while I sucked it raw, and I think his girlfriend saw it. I gave him a blow job at the whirlpool across from his dorm."

"Honey! You are on fire! What a dirty old hag you are! Tell me more!"

"Well, you know our unfortunate trouble this past Wednesday and he said he was too tired to do anything after practice. These were his exact words, 'too tired to make love to you the way I want to.' He didn't say fuck or screw he said, 'make love.' He said he wanted it to be the whole deal, the real thing."

Fielding puts her left hand on my arm and slaps her head with her right hand. "Jenna, for the love of all that is holy, will you relax with this guy? He's into you! Honestly, for someone who is so smart, who gives everyone else such good advice, you are absolutely daft when it comes to men, and especially with this one. He must be one hell of a stud as he's really thrown you off of your game. Look, even if he's not totally over his girlfriend, he will be after a night with you, and it didn't hurt that his ex saw you *in flagrante delicto*. Nothing says kaput to your relationship like your ex's cock in some other bitch's mouth."

"You should open a greeting card company or something. That's so lovely, and yet so true," I snort, driving down that troublesome old road.

We decide to go old-style slut for the concert—hoochie momma all the way. It's amazing how long it takes to pull off such a trashy, cheap look.

"Do you think my hair is big enough?" Fielding asks. Even without heels it appears she has grown a solid five inches.

"You always did have big, beautiful hair. It's gorgeous! I bow to you, rock goddess—80s video vamps ain't got nothing on you! Has Cliff ever seen you like that?" I point to the hot mess on her head. Fielding always did have an awesome head of hair. It's one of the few consistent things I love about her.

"Yeah, well, I was morphing out of it when we met at the beginning of grad school. A few days ago, though, I was experimenting with outfits and hair, and…well, I thought I'd never get it untangled. Did you know that Holdz-It hairspray and cum stick together like crazy?"

"Oh, that is a visual I did not need, Fielding!" I gasp, trying to catch my breath, doubled over at her admission. "How about a drink?"

"Is it my old favorite?"

"Of course! What else would it be?"

After the first singer's set, we head out to the

Volunteer Arena. Very quickly, I realize we are far from the only hoochie mommas. In fact, we are in a sea of hoochie mommas—emphasis on the *momma*. While the years have been kind to some, for many, the years have been hard—and droopy.

"Are you sure we're at the right concert?" Fielding asks.

I scrounge in my purse for the tickets, checking them. "Yup, we're right. This is it."

Fielding taps a lady on the shoulder. "Excuse me, are you here for Alice Cooper and Ozzie Osborne?" Her only response is a scowl.

"Fielding! You better watch out! You'll get your tall, scrawny ass kicked!"

Just as we are feeling superior, feeling like titanium, certain of our backstage-pass-worthy hotness, we round the corner and see them: the twenty-somethings. They are brunette and blonde and thin and smooth and tight and chic and new. They are perfect without trying, which is the definition of the young.

We both sigh at the sight. It's phenomenal and heartbreaking all at the same time because no matter how well you have aged, you know, at the end of the day you can't compete solely in the looks department—lucky for us. Experience breeds confidence, and confidence breeds sex appeal. We've got the goods and aren't afraid to put them out there. You just have to find that buyer who favors exquisite antiques.

"Don't let that get to you! We've got years of concert experience! " Fielding grabs my sleeve and leads me through the throng of Daisy-Duked ladies to our seats.

"Are these seats awesome or what?" I declare, proud

of my score.

"Oh! Jenna, I love you! You are simply the best!" Fielding squeals as the lights go down and a bass rift blares.

I know this song. I know this sexy, gruffly bass tagline like I know my own children. My childhood crush and the song that morphed me (via masturbation) into a full-fledged teenage horn dog: "Affair of the Heart" by Rick Springfield.

The lights flip up and the smoke clears, and there he stands above me—a god. He still looks good, damn good—in fact so good that I forget I was thinking about Collin five seconds ago. Rick's eyes are intensely scanning the audience, working us into a frenzy, his fingers nimbly caressing his guitar. I've heard this song a thousand times, but this one, this is the best. Feeding off of the crowd of horny, crazed, dazed, squalling women, Mr. Springfield's voice couldn't be any deeper or more luscious, full of passion. My knees are weak and I am burning for this man.

Fielding points and laughs at me, but I don't care. I could seriously faint—or die—and be perfectly happy. The only thing that would make it better would be Big Blue by my side, or…somewhere else.

"Are you gonna be okay?" She teases, buoying me with her arms under mine.

"He is so fucking hot! He is the hottest man on earth!" I wail, almost in tears.

"Hotter than Collin?"

"Yes!"

"Hotter than Travis?"

"Yes!"

"Hotter than my dildo?"

"Please don't make me answer that!"

We are five rows back, which isn't far off, but like a union lock-out, the competition is fierce to get to the stage. Fielding, an ex-volleyball player, is tall and muscular, her shoulders an impressive width, and she uses them with the skill of a police swat team, dragging my useless, trash-talking ass along with her.

By the time we muscle our way to the stage, one of Fielding's crushes, Billy Idol, is beginning his set with, "Dancing With Myself." I watch Fielding as she is mesmerized; her body is rhythmically moving in time with Idol's thrusting and gyrating. During one of his songs, I watch as one of the guitar players runs to the side of the stage and points our way—it could be any number of women—but it is not long before a short, chubby roadie-type dressed in black grabs Fielding's head and blesses her with the holy grail of rock concert regalia: the backstage pass.

"Hey! What about my friend? One for her?"

"Sorry! The Rock Gods were specific—you."

Out of the blue, a cat-eyed, pink-haired punk-of-a-girl lunges at Fielding, trying to wrestle the pass over the top of Fielding's Holdz-It-inflamed hair. I grab at the punk girl's shoulders and attempt to pull her off, but end up flat on my ass in a sea of short skirts and heels. Fielding, in the middle of the fray, kicks her mile-long legs at the throng of guards that has surrounded her.

"Jenna! Jenna! I'll meet you back at the hotel! Keep your cell phone on in case I get arrested!"

"OK! You do the same!" I sputter, drowning in the mob of estrogen that fills in our spots next to the stage.

I leave the concert early and hoof it back to the hotel, expecting to see Fielding very soon. But, hours pass and suddenly it is past midnight, and no sign of her, not a word. I am worried and what little sleep I can get is fractured, full of concern for her. I'm not as worried about her physical safety as I am about the safety of her heart.

At nearly five in the morning my cell ringing startles me out of a dream.

"Sorry. I tried knocking quietly, but I guess you didn't hear me. Can you let me in?"

Throwing my cell on the bed, I spring to the door and yank it open. Her hair is matted, and her mascara and eyeliner smudged across her face. When I review my best friend Fielding, I know what has happened.

Through thick heaving sobs and tears, she confesses while I hold her. "I'm so ashamed! I feel horrible! How could I have let that happen! What is Cliff going to think? He'll hate me, hate me, *hate* me! And the kids…oh the kids will hate me!"

"Fielding, tell me exactly what happened. Did he give you a drink or slip something to you?" I quiz, ruthlessly hunting for anything to help alleviate her guilt.

"Security was ready to throw me out, but I showed them my backstage pass and so they let me go right beside the stage door, and then I saw that guy, the one who gave me the pass from the stage. He escorts me back to the dressing area where there are other people. So, we're drinking and eating, having a great time watching the show from the backstage monitors, and the next thing I know, *he* is standing in front of me, talking to me just the way we are now. Then the party heats up, you know what I mean—booze, coke—all the regular rock n' roll party helpers. He starts making the rounds and I don't see him for a while, so I decide to leave because it's no fun without you. And that's when his ghoul, the guy from the stage, takes me out to the bus. He says, 'The Rock Gods would love to get to know you better, would you stay, please?' And then I meet him…he's all charming and polite, and convincing with his sexy accent, but Jenna, I knew, I *knew* what that meant, and still, I just sat there on my hands like a silly, stupid *girl*! I waited for maybe ten minutes and he steps on the bus—just the two of us." Her eyes tear up again and I see that in her mind, she is transported back to the days of high school fantasy. "He is so lovely, very soft spoken, freshly showered, he looks old and tired, and I suddenly feel really sorry for him. This is all he can do, and his body is tired, and he's alone after every show, I mean not *alone* alone, but not with anyone who really cares about him. He has no children; nothing tangible will be left of him when he's gone, and I ask him what makes him laugh, what makes him happy.

"He asks me about myself and I tell him that I used to be a massage therapist, and I ask him if he wants a foot massage. He's surprised, but says, 'Yeah, bloody good idea!' One thing leads to another and before I know it, we're making love. It's not the torrid, sweaty, drug-induced, orgy-like experience I had always imagined, but instead it was sweet and passionate and…I liked it." Fielding whispers the last sentence with her forehead cradled in her hand.

"Now what, Jenna? Now what?"

"I don't know."

Screaming, she unleashes her frustration on me. "What the hell do you mean you don't know? You're supposed to have all the fucking answers! You're the one that's older! You're older than me! You're supposed to know!" She slings her purse at me, pounding her fists in the bed. "Where were you? I needed you and you weren't there!"

Fielding collapses onto my lap and I drag her up into my arms where we sleep—not old, not young anymore, we are misfits. At one point in my life, I was on the receiving end of betrayal. I did not let it embitter me, but I have struggled to understand how it happens to people, especially good people like Fielding, people who appear to have found their pearl in a shell, sitting in the palm of their hands. And now, I understand. It's not anything you figure out with your brain; you have to use your heart. When I open my eyes, I see Fielding watching me. Her brown eyes are rimmed in red; she's clearly been crying again.

"Jenna, I don't want to go home. I can't go home and face Cliff. He'll know. He will hate me. He will take the children away from me."

I take a deep breath. *I really don't know whether my words will make any difference to her, but I must try because I simply cannot watch her self-destruct.* "Fielding, I don't know one marriage that doesn't go through a rough spot. If you choose to tell Cliff, you know he'll be hurt and angry, but he won't hate you. How could he hate you?"

"I'd hate him if he did it to me!"

"Would you, really?"

"Welll…No. I don't know, probably not. In fact, if he had been in a situation like mine, I'd probably just let him have a hall pass. I mean, it was a fantasy come true, and it was sweet, but it's not like I'm in love with the dude. We just had sex. Sex is sex, falling for someone else, that's worse, much worse. And lying about it is absolutely *the* worst."

"Sooner or later, everybody messes up; it's the human condition. No one is made of titanium—*no one*."

"What if I don't tell Cliff?"

"Then I will, you slut!" I joke.

"You're an asshole!" She jabs me in the arm. "Really, could you keep this secret with me, if I decide that's what I want to do?" She sits rocking back and forth, hugging her knees.

"Well, of course, of course. You know I would. This is not anything I would ever have a right to tell, anyway."

I watch as fresh tears roll across her leg and she reaches out, pressing her arms around mine. "You know what bothers me almost as much as disappointing Cliff?"

"No. What?"

"I'm afraid that I've disappointed you. Do you think I'm a total piece of shit?"

Smoothing her hair, I put my mouth close to her ear. "You know, this wise woman once told me she would never stoop to calling her friend a whore because she simply was acting like a woman with a man's morals."

This is the first genuine smile I've seen spread across her face since yesterday. I grab the phone. "Room service, please? I'd like two deluxe breakfasts delivered to room 5420, and bring extra coffee and a pitcher of mimosas, please."

"Oh, booze for breakfast! I don't think I deserve a treat," Fielding groans.

"It's to celebrate new beginnings—yours and mine."

Chapter Eleven

Ready or Not Here I Come

As much pain as Fielding has, I have even more for
her. Living with your mistakes is always harder than
confessing them, and I know she wants me to tell her
what she should do, but I can't, though I would do just
about anything to help relieve her of her guilt.

Despite her indiscretion, all I can think about when
I get home is seeing Collin. Finally, when Friday arrives,
I gleefully cut my day short as usual and drive like the
proverbial bat out of hell to drop off the kids. Collin
agrees to meet me at my house at four. We're cooking
dinner together—and I couldn't care less what the food
tastes like.

At a quarter to, I hear a rap on the door. Weighted
down with a bulging sack of groceries and a bottle of
wine, I watch him through the sidelight, nervously
waiting for me to open the door, his sweaty hands
marking the brown paper bag; he marks time and
awkwardly scratches his legs with his feet. While he is
pushing his glasses back up his nose, I rip open the door,
startling him.

I try not to smile too much. "Oh, it's you! Well, I
had no clue."

"Were you trying to make me wait? Don't you think
I've waited long enough?" His eyes peek through his

long bangs and immediately, I feel warm and tingly—warm and tingly exactly where a woman *wants* to feel when she's with a man she simply must have.

Without breaking our eye contact, I glide very close to him, scooping the sack from his arms. I settle it on the floor and we collapse into a heap beside it, our tongues and hands knowing no boundaries. He doesn't ask me about my weekend, or my week, or about the kids, or dinner; he doesn't say anything else to me. He kisses me; his mouth is perched softly on mine, gooey hot spit sliding off of our tongues, onto our lips. He pushes hard into me—his whole body is tense and vibrating with excitement. His breath is shallow and comes in quick spurts.

He whispers, "Do you want an hors d'oeuvre before we start making dinner?"

I nod and he pulls the grocery bag over. Out tumbles a loaf of French bread, baby spinach, cherry tomatoes, a stick of Irish butter, a bunch of parsley, a scallion, baking chocolate, strawberries *with* the stems, whipping cream, red wine, and two steaks—plus a large box of magnums. He tosses the box aside and runs to put the rest of the food in the refrigerator.

"Wow! When you said cook dinner, you really meant it," I struggle to get the words out, my brain pulling me away from everything that is domestic, everything that is not him.

"I want this to be perfect, Jenna. You deserve something perfect."

Before I can catch my breath, he pulls me to my feet and leads me to the living room floor. Spreading a blanket wide on the floor, he drops to his knees in front of me, lifting up my shirt and pulling my bare stomach to his mouth. Slowly, he unbuttons and unzips my shorts, his lips pouring soft kisses down my thighs—down to my knees, around to the back of my thigh, back to the zipper, which he opens all the way. My shorts fall to the floor; I won't need those for the rest of the evening, I'm sure.

Down on my knees now, I let the thin straps of my tank top topple down my shoulders. He plunges his tongue—a wet kiss—on either bare shoulder, yanking my tank over my head. Against my tan skin, the light pink lacy bra and panties look almost white; his heavy breath is audible now and with his hands around my waist, I increase my breath to match his. He relays a scorching passion for me that I interpreted from the first time his blue eyes laid claim to me.

I am perfectly *his* tonight.

Our mouths find each other again and I am shaking so much that the button on his shorts seems an impossible task. I strip him of all of his clothes and my hands trace over every inch of his body that I can reach. He is firm and his skin is soft. His cock is so hard that my knees wobble at the thought of what will happen next.

"Come here, in the kitchen," he requests, leading me in front of him. "Do you have a deep bowl and a mixer?" he asks, his hardness teasing my ass.

I can hardly think, yet I do remember where they are; I point to the cabinet in the kitchen island.

He pulls the whipping cream out of the fridge and sets up the bowl under the mixer stand. "Here. Stand in front of me. We're going to make whipped cream—the real thing. It's the best, don't you think?"

Again, all I can do is nod and do as I'm told,

standing in front of him. He positions himself behind me and rests his head on my shoulder, swiping my hair around to one side. With his foot he spreads my legs apart and wraps a strong arm around my waist. Pressing into me with his hard on, he turns the mixer to start and slowly grinds into my ass, the mixer on the lowest speed. He grabs my hand and puts it inside his, his moist hand clamping down on mine that rests on my soft stomach.

As the mixer speed increases, so does his grinding and thrusting. He slips his hand into my pink panties and massages my clit, slowly moving his fingers to the wet hot lips of my honey pot. The blood wildly courses through them; I am on the verge of an incredible orgasm and I shift my pelvis in the hope that his fingers will slip inside of me. He alternates kisses and bites on my neck and shoulder.

Suddenly, the mixer is silent. With his busy little fingers he slides out of my panties, he scoops a dollop of whipped cream and holds it to my lips. I do the same for him.

"Is it sweet enough without sugar?" I ask.

"You know it is, baby."

We take ourselves—and our bowl—to our blanket. I yank him down on me and our lips and tongues are frantic; he yanks my panties to the floor and viciously unhooks my bra.

I desperately part my lips with his cock in one gulp, letting him thrust in my mouth, wanting him to shoot his sticky load of cum down my throat. He stops me and straddles me—sixty-nine—Collin's face on my mound and his dick deep in my throat. A cold, frothy substance surprises me—he's spread a mound of whipped cream on my clit. The tip of his tongue dances across it until I moan with that familiar wave of contentment. Collin flips around and coats my tits with the cream and slowly licks them clean; my nipples are hard buds, and I want him so badly that I ache.

"Kiss me, baby! I want to taste my pussy on your mouth." I grab the back of his head, pulling him to me, and don't waste a single drop. "Collin, I want you now! I want you to pound me until I scream because there is nothing else I want more than to bend over and let you give it to my ass like a bad girl."

With trembling hands, he slides on the magnum while I roll on my back, listening to my heart thump uncontrollably, barely able to wait for his sweet hot love to unfold inside of me. He does not need my guidance. He knows exactly where to go and how to get there. We both moan in splendid agreement at the first few tight strokes, my sweet juice coating his fat cock. Collin's face is pink, flushed with excitement; he hauls the air out of his lungs slowly, deeply gasping with every plunge. I snatch onto his perfect pole, my sugar walls repeatedly collapsing around it.

"More! I need more—again! Don't stop!" I demand.

He clamps his hands around my face, forcing me to keep my eyes open, to watch him watching me. I close my legs under him, my clit swelling. Pushing my hands down on his ass, he pumps harder, moving his thumb to my mouth. I suck it and open my mouth, gulping for air.

"I want you to come for me, baby. I *need* you to come," he whispers in my ear, tracing my earlobe and my wet lips with his tongue.

Throwing my head back, my chest heaves and my muscles tense, wanting this with him like I've never wanted anything else, and surpassing those wicked orgasms of my fantasies.

"Oh! Col-lin, Col-lin! Yeah baby! I'm coming! Oh, your fuck is so good!" I jerk his face to mine and our tongues slip and grind while he pounds it home.

He has the most serious look on his face that I've ever seen. I think, *Is he going to continue to screw me or hit me?* We're both drenched in sweat, our bodies hot to the touch—and we don't stop. He makes me come two more times before pulling me to my knees.

"I *love* doggy style," I groan, arching my back and pushing my ass into his hands. He gives it a firm squeeze, followed by wet kisses that leave me breathless and tingly. With his hands he gently splays my legs further apart and enters me. From this position, I feel his true breadth; it spreads me apart and I almost yelp in discomfort, but taking a deep breath, I relax, my juices flowing again. I hear the sloppy wetness of my hole.

He grunts, "Damn. You've got such a tight pussy, and it sounds so good when I fuck it. Can you hear that? Can you hear my fat cock fucking your pretty, wet pussy, baby? Oh, Jenna, fuck me back—hard!"

With my ass slapping hard against his solid thighs, I barely have time to come one last time before he explodes. He digs his fingers into my hips, groaning and grunting his pleasure; with every final stroke, he heaves a cry of relief. I look back over my shoulder, grinning at the expression on his face. He is completely satisfied— and so am I.

"I can't think of any other place I'd rather be right now. This is perfect, right here," he confesses, never taking me from his blue-eyed stare.

"Not even if you could be on the block at the swim competition, getting that gold medal?

"Ah, only if you're there and you promise to do to me what you just did as soon as I'm off the block."

We lie content next to each other, dozing, under the drone of the ceiling fan. He rolls over to face me, whispering in my ear, "You hungry? I'd love to make you dinner—before we go another round."

I don't have to tell him that I'm starving, or that I'm scared—*I'm scared out of my freaking mind at the way he is making me feel.*

"You didn't tell me you were a master chef," I compliment him later over dinner, blushing at his full-on stare at me, which doesn't ever seem to stop.

"You're so beautiful, you know that? I can't believe you're forty. You look ten years younger, easy, maybe more. It's no wonder Travis didn't want to let you go. I could get used to this, waking up next to your pretty face. Do you think you'll ever get married again?"

The question rocks me to my core. I'm surprised, scared, excited, and concerned. It's too early in the relationship to be thinking, or even *talking* about this, and he's too young. He's supposed to be planning dates and going out with his friends and all the things you do when you're young, single, and childless: when things are so much less complicated. You don't go complicating simple.

"Well, I don't know. Well, yeah, I *do* know." I finish my steak and head him off before he lets his mind wander any more. "I don't really think I ever want to get married again, and for that matter, I don't really think it's necessary. I mean, I've got the kids and friends, and…" I let my voice trail. *I'm not sure I should say it—you. Should I say that I've got him?* "I've got a great *beginning* with you. It all seems pretty perfect to me right now."

He chases a chunk of steak with the rest of his wine. I sense the wind-up in his mind, the questions, the things I'm not sure I'm prepared to discuss with him, or know how to discuss with him.

"So, you've ruled it out entirely? You'll never do it again, at all?" He doesn't try to hide the disappointment that runs down his face as he waits.

"No, I'm not ruling it out completely—never say never. Isn't that what they say? But, it would have to be exactly the right situation, the perfect person."

"Jenna, do you believe in fate, in just knowing when something is right?"

"I used to, but I'm not sure anymore when it comes to love. Collin, I just don't know. I thought I was deeply in love once—fairy tale stuff—and then it ended. The relationship ended up being painful and disappointing, and I think I'm a little jaded, to be honest, and very guarded when it comes to my heart."

"You don't think you could be in love like that again, not even with someone who adores you?"

"I still believe in love, but maybe, love like that is not out there for me again." I sit back and exhale deeply watching his face crease in thought. I don't want to believe that he is falling in love with me. That's not hot and sexy and impulsive. That's scary grown-up stuff, and I don't want any part of it right now.

He shifts in his seat and the oddest grin crosses his lips. "The night you had me over for dinner with your kids, I kept watching you with your kids and thought how great it would be to have that. You have a pretty nice life."

"You know, I also have baggage—three kids, and I

really don't want any more. What if we got married and you decided you wanted a child of your own, and I didn't or couldn't have one? You could resent me for the rest of your life, or be miserable, or maybe I might get sick and you'd have to take care of me! That'd suck!" I lay my face in my hands, wishing we could push the rewind button on this conversation. "I don't want to talk about this anymore, okay? We're having an awesome evening. Let's not ruin it." I punctuate my sentence with annoyance.

He pushes back into his seat, surprised at my tone. *Great! Now you've done it. You've treated him like a child instead of like the kind of man any sane woman would want to be with.*

"You don't have to be upset about it, or with me. I'm not trying to pressure you, but I want to be honest with you. I don't know any other way to be. Remember? Do those words sound familiar, Jenna?" he reaches over and strokes my hair, rubbing his face in it, softening his tone to a whisper, "Sweetheart, I can't help how I feel. I can't choose who moves me, but I can choose what to do with it. I'm not asking you to marry me. I'm just asking for you to give me a chance to make you fall in love with me."

My eyes unexpectedly well up with tears and I decide to welcome this freedom back: the freedom to love. Laughing at myself, I answer, "You had me at 'hey'."

"Ha! Yeah, that night I first talked to you. I had to do it, but I was so nervous I couldn't say anything else." He wipes the tears off of my face with his fingers.

"Well, as it turns out, you didn't have to. So, what's for dessert?" I run my hand up his leg to his balls, offering them a good squeeze.

He stands up, his stiff cock facing my lips. "Me."

I bend over to lick the tip, teasing him. Leaving him throbbing and wanting more, I strut over to grab the bowl of whipped cream, and I snag the strawberries out of the refrigerator.

"Help me make this, would you, baby?" I purr.

"I'll do anything you want me to, sweetie."

"Get the baking chocolate and let's melt it.

"Do you have a glass bowl or something?" he asks.

"Uh-uh." I wag my finger at him. "That's boring. We're not doing that. We're going to melt it with our body heat. Come here."

I unwrap the bar and press it against my stomach, reaching for him. He presses firmly against me, my tits mash up against his chest. As the chocolate softens its fragrant vanilla and cocoa scent funnels up between us.

I grab a strawberry, aware of his eyes resting heavily on me, his mouth open in anticipation, rubbing his hardness into my soft, hot, wet spot. He steals the strawberry out of my hand, dips it in our melting chocolate, then the whipped cream, and offers it to me. Instead of feeding me though, he pulls it away, teasing me, and offers his lips, which I greedily taste with my tongue. I duck my face left and right, trying not to let him kiss me. He has to work for it. With his hand on the nape of my neck, he ravishes my lips, diving to my stomach and forging a path through the chocolate with his strong tongue. Collin finally puts the strawberry between us and we share it.

"You are one sexy motherfucker!" I gasp, nearly ready to explode.

"You've not seen anything yet. Let's go get a

shower. I want to ask you something."

My heart races and I wonder what he wants to ask me. Hoping it's not a rehash of our earlier conversation, I follow him up the steps, shaking. He glances back at me with a sly smile, a smile I can't decode. He points to me, laughing.

"You've got chocolate all over your face!" He grabs his side and rests his head on my shoulder, giggling.

"Well, you do, too! I guess you could say we've got a couple of shit-eating grins on our faces!" I snort and grab him, still curious. "Say, what is it that you want to ask me?"

Collin dips to one knee and my stomach plummets out from under me, and my knees begin to wobble uncontrollably. My arms break out in goosebumps. Gently lifting my left hand into his, he asks, "Do you remember what you said to me earlier, right before we started making love?"

"I...I don't know." Confused, I struggle to remember.

"You said 'I want you to pound my pussy until I scream because there is nothing else I want more than to bend over and give it to my ass like a bad girl.' Do you remember that?"

"Yeah..." I shudder from the top of my head to my toes, getting the drift of where this conversation is going.

"I want to do that, Jenna. Could we do that? I've never done it before, and I want to, with *you*, *please*?" He squeezes my hips and kisses my tummy, giving it one last promising lick, searing my entire body with his scorching hot promise.

Anal intercourse, butt-fucking, up the butt, butthole surfing, corn-holing, fudge-packing—whatever you want to call it—that particular brand of sex eventually raises its head in every relationship. For most women, it's a curiosity, tempered with some healthy fear, to be tried at least once, with the *right* guy. For men, it's the sexiest, dirtiest, I'm-the-king-of-all-cocks stuff of fantasies. And thanks to porn, men believe they all should be able to do it, and that all women should be thrown to the top of the orgasm scale when it happens. What men don't understand is this: It's not a stick-it-in-and-go procedure, like quickies sometimes can be. It takes time; it takes trust, and a seriously hot connection with your partner; *and* it takes some serious lube—a lot of it.

Although I am up for doing whatever Collin wants, I am also aware of this little-talked-about female concern when it comes to anal sex: The slut factor. It seems you never outgrow this one. *Will he think I am a nasty, porn-type slut if I let him do me in the butt?* For the record, I believe most guys will *not* think you are a nasty, porn-type slut if you give in to anal sex. They will most likely think you are a hot lay who is exponentially turned on by their sexual prowess because you allow them to violate you in such a hot, dirty, perverted way. It doesn't hurt if you play up your inexperience; that makes it seem even more wrong and perverted. That is head-bobbing, high-fiving, secret-bragging-rights shit for most men.

"Collin, I've only done it once. It happened organically."

He greets me with a confused, disappointed glare. "So, does that mean you don't want to do it, or you do?"

"No, what I mean is that every time I've ever planned it, it hasn't worked. You'll have to be really, *really* patient. Okay?"

"Oh, I will be, I promise. I will be *soooo* patient. Did you like it when you did it before?"

"Yeah, it was really intense, and a very different feeling, but…"

"What?" He scours my eyes for concern.

"Well, you're kind of big—thick. I'm afraid it might hurt. I don't know whether it will work."

"Do you trust me?"

"Yeah."

"Then let me take care of you, let me have your ass, baby," he whispers in my ear, and then flips me over, his ramrod cock driving the strength of his desire home to me right in the small of my back.

"Take me."

We clean each other in the shower, taking our time, letting our hands, tongues, and minds explore each other freely, our minds absorbed in giving the other unselfish pleasure. Collin dries me off and slathers my body with lotion, taking long thoughtful strokes down my arms, legs, and back.

He escorts me to bed, where we kiss and continue to explore for a millennium—lips, eyes, hair, arms, breasts, backs, legs, breasts, nipples. He wraps himself around my body, enveloping me, making love, and leading me to the edge of satisfaction.

"You still trust me?" He asks, anticipation dripping off of his voice.

My lips are dry. He kisses me. "Yes. I do."

I flip to my back and spread my legs open for him, ready for this experience. He watches me, watching him ready himself, pouring a generous handful of the lube in his palm, stroking himself—and me.

At first, frustrated beads of sweat pop out over his

forehead. He stops for a moment, trumpeting air through his disheartened lips.

"Sometimes, it takes a little while," I explain, stroking his arm. "Please, be patient with me. You said you would, remember?"

"I know. I just didn't think it'd be this challenging," he says, his head hanging in defeat.

"No! It takes *time*! Work with me, play with me some more, make me beg for it," I smile, tracing my finger along his chiseled jawline.

He smiles back at me and takes me to the limits of sanity with his tongue, fingers, and cock.

"Please, Collin! Take it now before I go crazy!" I beg, clawing at his arms and hands.

He pours lube on himself and me, massaging it in carefully. Grabbing me by my thighs, he wrenches my bottom up as close to his cock as possible and pushes up on me. As the tip pops in, we collectively breathe a sigh of relief, and he begins his slow, shallow rhythmic pumping. I flinch and try to pull back, pushing off against his arms

"No, don't pull away—relax. Just take a deep breath and look at me. Tell me what you need with your eyes—too fast, too slow, too deep, stop?"

I wrap my fingers around his wrists, breathing deeply, thinking how gorgeous he is with his face flushed and sweaty, his bangs sweeping over one eye. He accelerates his pumping, using only the most controlled force. He watches my chest expand and deflate as I draw in deep breaths. And, finally, I relax.

"I'm *in*! Baby this is so hot!" he yelps, almost as excited as my kids were when we went to the amusement park last year.

I tighten the grip on his wrists, begging, "Do it! Do it baby!"

With longer, fluid strokes, he does exactly what I told him to do: he gives my ass what it craves, and I love every second of it. I see stars. I hear a chorus of church bells. I cannot get close enough to him, or drink up enough of that entranced, lustful gaze on his face.

I walk my fingers down my stomach, rubbing and tapping my clit, following his eyes as they study me, winding me up inside until our cravings completely intoxicate our bodies.

"Fuck! This is amazing Jenna! I want you to tell me when you're ready to come."

"Honey, this is so hot."

Together, we scream and groan, indulging in every last pulse of pleasure that echoes in our bodies. We finally pull apart from one another, crushingly exhausted, and very, *very* satisfied.

I don't know how many times we replay our Friday night follies for the rest of the weekend, but I know this: I am so tired Monday morning that I do not hear my alarm clock go off. My kids shake me from a deep sleep and a bolt of panic rushes through me at the sound of the school bus brakes. *Ah, back to reality.*

****

Wanting to catch up with Fielding, I surprise her with lunch at her office. In the confines of her tiny cubicle, I relay my prurient misbehavior of the weekend.

"Damn! In the name of all that is good and right, you are one bad-ass cougar. If he lives to be a hundred years old, he will never, *ever*, forget the time he spent with you."

"Well, there is only one problem I see with it all,

though."

"What could possibly be problematic about great sex, great food cooked by your young lover, and an amazing fuck up your ass?" Fielding asks straight-faced, a thickly buttered roll poised at her lips.

I sputter uncontrollably, my fist pounding on the table. "You really know how to put things in perspective for a girl, don't you?" People are beginning to pop their heads out of cubicles, gopher-style.

"Well, that's my job. I'm your best friend. So, really, what is eating you, Goober Grape?"

"I'm scared of the way he makes me feel, or really, the feelings that he's stirring up in me, feelings I think I have told myself that I won't have, can't have again."

"Like love?"

"Yeah, like love. He asked me if I thought I'd ever get married again and I told him I didn't really think I would. I said, 'I think it's unnecessary'."

"Ouch! That was a poor choice of words. Kinda cold, ma'am."

"Yeah, well, it doesn't get better. At one point, I told him I didn't want to talk about it anymore."

"Yup, that is a lot worse. Did he leave?"

"No, he stayed and very calmly asked for a chance to make me fall in love with him. Then, he screwed me silly for the rest of the weekend."

"Jenna, I love you, but you're the stupidest person I've ever seen. Listen, honey, I'm only going to say this once: Go for it! If he wants a chance at making you love him then let it happen. I know you're scared, but not all guys are like your ex, Paul. In fact, he's in a class of asshole all by himself. I'm pretty sure of it."

"You're right. It would be nice to be in love again,

to have…well what you have."

Fielding tears up and clenches my arm. "Jenna, I can tell you from experience that there is nothing more important than love. Is there *anything* more important than love, except maybe outstanding anal sex?" She giggles and shakes her hands in front of her, negating her addition. "Great sex is great, but it's no competition for love. Don't miss out on something good because you're afraid."

I shake my head in agreement, arguing, "But what about our age difference? I can foresee all sorts of problems with that. What if he wants a baby and I don't or can't? What if I get sick and he has to take care of me? What if his parents and friends hate me? What if my kids hate him?"

"Love is never guaranteed to be easy, but you'll never know if you don't do it. Let me put it this way, honey." She smiles like a minx.

"Just get on with it, Dr. Fielding."

"Jenna, don't overthink love because when you're *in* love, sometimes you just gotta say fuck it."

"Girl, I have said that many, many times over the past few months."

"Yeah, but you've got to be willing to do it. Go big or go home."

My eyes dart slyly at her and I ask, "You up for another trip?"

She rolls her eyes. "I don't know. You might want to ask Cliff about that."

"Why? Did you tell him about Nashville?"

"Nah, but I've come close. I think he knows. I'm acting a little weird."

"That's just in your head. He doesn't know

anything. Just stuff those feelings, make whatever religious restitution you need to make, and forget it happened."

"Billy is so cute!" she coos, running her nail over a picture of him she put in a little frame on her desk.

"Fielding! Stop! Would you like to go to Kansas City with me to watch Collin in the World Swim Competition trials?"

"Hell yeah! Hot, young, ripped dudes…"

"Wet, tight swim trunks…we'll have to leave on Sunday. Paul has the kids for a week—summer break."

"Duh! Twist my arm! But, don't try to cockblock my good time."

"Hey, that's fine, but don't be pissed when you do something you regret, again, and want me to fix it, again, and then I can't."

"You're a cold bitch, but a smart one. I'm glad I've got you."

"Let's go to Kansas City!"

Chapter Twelve

For the Love of Beefcake

While I've never really liked the Midwest, and am not much of a frequent beef eater, I am compelled to admit that I am an avid fan of the *beefcake*, of which there is *a lot* in Kansas City during the World Swim Competition trials. It is an amazing smorgasbord of young, hot dudes running around in their skivvies, usually wet and breathless. It leaves Fielding and me wet and breathless, too.

"Oh, screw me stupid! Do you see all of this? Why did you bring me here? This is like bringing a drug addict to a cocaine and pill-themed Hollywood party! Do you see all the guys here? Do you see the ripped abs, nice packages, and tight asses neatly shoved in their snug little swim shorts? It makes the nine-hour trip soooo worth it."

"Fielding, I think you need to close your mouth. It's hanging open! Of course, I have no room to talk. I believe I may have just caught a fly or two."

"Ha! It will be a miracle if I can go one day, no, one *hour* without screwing myself silly with my dildo," Fielding groans.

"You brought your dildo?" I gasp.

"Well, yeah. You *didn't*?"

"I figured I didn't need to bring it," I gloat. "What if

116

the hotel maid sees it?"

Fielding punches my arm. "I'm pretty sure she won't touch it. Hey, hey, hey! Isn't that..." She points across the room and my eyes follow her finger.

At the corner of the coach's table is a familiar face—Travis. His blond hair and blue eyes harpoon me, dragging my mood down to the bottom of the pool. Ex-lover radar is uncanny; when you least expect it, when everything else is chugging along, full steam ahead, a sudden blockade appears on the track, and there's no way around it. You've got to get out, confront the problem, and move the damn thing out of the way. I honestly didn't believe I would see Travis again for a while, at least not until the kids begin swim lessons again in the fall.

My heart thumps in my chest as his head bobs up and his eyes make direct contact with mine. He's not changed much—still easy on the eyes and I instantly, involuntarily replay all of our times together. Without a doubt, I know his wave is for me.

"Okay, you keep an eye out for Collin. I don't want him to see me talking to Travis. I'm afraid it might throw him off of his game."

"He's something else, Jenna. Are you sure you're done with him?" Fielding inquires, licking her chops.

"Yeah, I have to be if I'm going to be with Collin."

"Go get 'im girl, oh, and good luck with trying to ignore all those old feelings creeping up in your coochie."

"Fielding!"

I weave my way through the throng of swimmers. I warn myself, *I must be titanium. Things are good, no* great *with Collin and messing this up puts me at a disadvantage.* For good measure, I replay Fielding's advice: *There is nothing more important than love.*

"Hey you!" I reach out to touch his shoulder and he goes in for a hug—a long hug that leaves me reeling with his familiar scent wrapped around me. I push away, blushing. "I didn't know you'd be here. Are you competing?"

"Nah, I'm coaching, well, helping to coach—assistant to the assistant. I figure it would look good on my resume. You've got to start somewhere. It's really good to see you, Jenna. You look great, really. Really great—happy."

An awkward pause languishes between us. I know what he means—he misses me, but understands that I'm with someone else—for now. "Yeah, things are good, we're…doing well."

"I guess you're here to see Rat Boy, uh, I mean Collin." He grins widely, hiding his mischievous smile under his coach badge. "Listen, I want to apologize for all that. It was stupid, and immature, and I'm sorry. I know we can't be friends, but at least we can be friendly?" His eyes search mine for forgiveness and all I can think of is the first time I rode him in the back of my van. He has exactly the same expression on his face.

"Oh, Travis, of course we'll be friendly. We're fine, really, we are. I know you were upset. I understand, totally. Thank you, though, for the apology. I appreciate it." Unexpectedly, I reach out to rub his elbow, moving my hand further up to his shoulder, letting it linger there.

He covers my hand with his. "I miss you, Jenna. God, I miss you so much.

"Travis, I…"

"You don't have to say anything. I just wanted you

to know that, just in case. I've got to go. Bye."

Out of the corner of my eye I see two things: Collin walking out for his turn in the prelims and Fielding, pouncing on a leftover treat—Travis. It's not that I mind, because if there's ever someone who would be worth it, it would be him, but I feel a little guilty and responsible for dragging her here. If I had known she was bent on self-destruction, I would not have invited her. *One mistake, life goes on. Two mistakes, life can start to get a little screwy; shame on me for not buoying her up when she needs it most.*

Watching Collin peel off his warm-up suit, I am aware of my insides knotting up, nervously watching him flex and stretch his arms. He takes his place on the block, pulling on his goggles and cap, and folds himself into position. I hold my breath, waiting for the buzzer.

I jump at the jarring noise, standing on my tippy toes to follow him with my eyes. He is a magnificent sight— arms stretched wide, plowing through the water, all of his strength and intensity channeled into one goal. It makes me want to do bad things to my muffin watching him, until I'm nudged back into reality.

"Hey! How'd your boy do?"

"Mmm—don't know yet. They haven't announced. So, I see you introduced yourself to Travis. You're a regular little welcome wagon aren't you?"

"Yeah, I might be. Are you *jealous*?"

"No, but what was all that shit about love being the most important thing?"

"For you, Jenna, not for me. You deserve that."

"What do you mean?"

"I asked Cliff for a trial separation. I've got a lot of crap I need to deal with, a lot of feelings that I need to either dump or embrace, and I just can't do it while I'm living with him. So, we agreed to separate for a while. He was surprisingly cool about it."

"Where are you going to live? Who's going to keep the kids?"

"Oooh! Look! They're posting the results. Let's talk about this some other time. Oh, and by the way, whenever you introduce me, my name is F.H. Fielding—call me F.H."

"What does F.H. mean?"

"Fucking hot."

Fielding dismisses my other questions, instead concentrating on the tally board.

Through clenched fists, I peek at the board, my heart sinking. He is five hundredths of a second too slow to be included in the semifinal heats. In a world of extremes, it is amazing how such a subtle difference can change the course of your whole life.

Rolling his head in disappointment, Collin's eyes find mine and he offers me a deflated smile. I know he is young and has many years to compete, but my heart breaks for him all the same because all he can see right now is the failure, not the future.

He slowly drags himself over to me, lowering his face to my shoulder. "Shit."

"It's okay, baby. You did awesome. I'm so proud of you! You can train and come back. There are guys here in their thirties competing. You can do that! You can…"

Collin presses his finger to my lips, and I am quiet. He whispers in my ear, "All I want to do right now is make love to you. I want to melt into you and forget about all of this for a while."

As we scurry out, I catch Fielding's eye, giving her

my plans with indecent sign language. She is flirting with some of the swimmers and coaches. I silently hope *her* subtleties and *her* extremes balance each other out.

****

Collin has dissolved into tears by the time we get back to my room, and my words and advice seem to be completely useless. I have never seen him so vulnerable; I've never seen *any* man so vulnerable. And it is making me hot for him like I've never been hot for anyone before—the promise he made to me that day at the party has been fulfilled.

"Hey now, sweetheart! Collin, please don't cry. Look at me—please. You know you did your best. You did what so few people do, and you'll go back to do it again. I know you will. You have so much ahead of you, not just swimming, but everything."

He pulls me to him and kisses my forehead, tracing my features, barely grazing my flesh. My skin swells with goose bumps and I hear my breath catch, and I close my eyes. Standing in front of him, my fingers play with the frayed edge of his t-shirt. I slide my hands around his rib cage, then to the small of his back, rappelling upwards until I am wrapping my fingers around his shoulders and peeling his shirt off of him. The damp hair at the nape of his neck still smells of chlorine. I inhale deeply, letting his scent penetrate my whole body.

"You are absolutely the most amazing man I've ever met," I whisper in his ear, tracing the lobe with my tongue.

"Please, I need to be inside of you," he cries softly.

I reach down to his pants, tracing the outline of his hardness with trembling fingers. Our clothes fall in a flurry to the floor and we barely make it to the bed as he sinks into me. As we both cry out, he swells and I buck beneath him treading passion until we finally dive head first into ecstasy. When he explodes inside of me, our eyes meet, and we exchange a thousand thoughts without uttering a single word.

He spoons me for the remainder of the afternoon, casting his ideas to me out loud, rolling strands of my hair between his fingers until we fall asleep.

I wake to long shadows on the floor, and to Collin's eyes exploring me. Smiling at him, I ask, "Are you alright?"

"Yeah, I'm okay. I'm sorry about the whole ridiculous crying thing."

"Oh, honey, don't even think it's necessary to apologize. We're past that point. You know, I care about you so much and when you hurt, I do, too. I understand the result you got today is not the one you wanted, but that doesn't mean it won't happen in the future, right?"

"Yeah, that's true. If I want it badly enough, and when the time is right, it will happen. But there's only one flaw I can find in your thinking."

I furrow my brow at him, perplexed. "What do you mean?"

"How can our sex possibly be any better than it was today?"

"Let me show you," I coo in his ear, disappearing under the sheets.

My mouth finds him—hard. As my tongue circles his shaft, my pulse reverberates in my body, concentrated in one solitary spot. His moans energize me and I am suddenly caught by his rugged arms diving under the sheets and wrenching me up to him.

He flips me on my stomach, under his virile body

and hoists my arms out straight, above my head, as he is slowly kissing my neck and shoulders, leaving me in a smoldering frenzy. I raise my backside and press into him. And when I do, he sweeps his arm under my front, holding me up.

With his legs, he spreads mine and enters me. Slowly, his hand moves from my stomach to my button—the one he is so excellent at pushing. With every languid stroke, I hear him winding up inside. I anxiously listen to his breath—heavy, dark velvet draping me in passion. There is no escape from under him and I remain motionless, in full joy, allowing him to do what he will. I am a very happy prisoner. The only sound in the room is our bodies slapping together, pounding out that beautiful, promising beat. And then we both tense for the avalanche of ecstasy, his warm excited explosion drenches my back.

"Do you have enough energy to go to dinner tonight? I'd like to see my teammates," Collin sputters, very nearly out of energy.

"Yeah, after a shower," I sigh, helplessly trying to repel all these feelings of…love.

****

Hand-in-hand, Collin and I walk to the hotel lobby to wait for his teammates. When the elevator doors open, Fielding and Travis are standing very close together, nearly head-to-head.

"Hey you!" she exclaims, her eyes cutting back to Travis. He bypasses Collin and me without a glance our way, heading out the door to the street.

"So, what's going on?" I ask, my eyes trailing Travis, afraid of the answer I might get from her.

"Oh, not much," she answers, looping a curl around

her finger. "I was upstairs with the team—Travis, the other coaches, the guys—you know—orgy."

"You should have called me! You look awesome, and not at all like you just participated in a naughty gangbang. I'm surprised you're not more exhausted."

"It was clean fun, Jenna—no alcohol, no sex, but I know what you're thinking about stud muffin out there." She rolls her eyes and tilts her head toward Travis.

"No, no, well, yeah I guess I was. Listen, I'm not trying to judge you. You do whatever you want with anyone you want, including Travis. All I ask is that you do what makes you *happy* because you're my best friend, and I love you, Fielding. I hope you know that."

She stands stone-faced, and I want her to lift her limp arms to hug me, but she doesn't. Instead, she unleashes her tirade. "How do you think it makes me feel that my husband, my *husband* is perfectly fine with my leaving? Hell, he practically helped me pack my bags. Give me one good reason why I shouldn't just happily join the cheater's club?" Her chest heaves with anger and hurt. She's on the verge of tears.

"Fielding, go and talk to Cliff! Leave now and go back to Kinweld—to him— and tell him everything. Get things sorted out. I can't read Cliff's mind!" I yell back.

"Things are not that cut and dried, Jenna! If you weren't so busy chasing after your boy toys we could have a really helpful conversation." She stomps across the lobby and out the door into darkness.

Suddenly, I feel very foolish and selfish. *Have I been so occupied satisfying my urges that I've forgotten my best friend's needs?*

Collin wanders back over to me and brushes my shoulder with his hand. "You alright? What was that all about?"

"Uh, I don't know. She's unhappy and I don't know what to do to help her."

Collin stands in front of me with his hands in his pockets, studying Fielding and Travis standing under the portico of the hotel. Shrugging his shoulders, he says, "Well, maybe the question you ought to be asking yourself is *can* you help her? Sometimes, you've just got to let people go do their own thing. She'll come back. You two are too close for anything else to happen." He seals his wise words with a kiss to my cheek.

"There you go with that smart thing again. How do you do that?"

"Aw, must be the company I keep. Come on, let's go find the yahoos and have dinner."

With my hand on my heart, I announce, loudly enough for anyone who wants to hear me, "You're brilliant! Simply brilliant!" I laugh deeply as he pulls me out the door.

A woman's power of persuasion is simply amazing. The Greeks have a saying: The man is the head of the family, but the woman is the neck, and she can turn the head any way she wants. My ex-father-in-law, a two-time divorcee, shaked his head when any discussion turns to relationships, remarking, "It's amazing what you'll do for a little patch of hair." Fielding and I call it Poontain Power. But, it's not just about your honey pot. It's an intangible mixture of charm, confidence, and intelligence, with a very tangible, "patch of hair" thrown in to seal the deal. If you've ever wanted something from a man, most likely you've figured out how to get it—and very quickly.

After dinner, all the girls want to go dancing, and the

guys agree to go too, because, well, they've been overcome by the power—Poontain Power.

Fielding and I sit at opposite ends of the table at the club, as we did at dinner, and I do not anticipate a thaw in the foreseeable future.

While Collin and I slow dance, I spy Fielding doing shots with Travis. She is tall, and meets his drunken glaze eye-to-eye as they hollow out a spot on the dance floor. She has one hand on the back of his neck, playing with his hair and ear, and the other stuck in his back pocket. As he grinds into her, she throws her head back, pulling him in for a passionate kiss on her neck.

Soon, the tempo of the music escalates, and so does the heat between Fielding and Travis. Ignoring the beat, they station themselves in one spot, kissing and grinding, their tongues and hands knowing no public decency. She relocates her hand from his back pocket to the front, rubbing his stiff cock. Travis slides his hands over Fielding's ass, giving it a good squeeze, then moves to the small of her back, and finally, around to her front, giving her tits the equal action he's offering to her ass.

I'm not sure either one of them knows what is happening by the time the manager slinks over to separate them, as they are so drunk on booze and horny. With a standing ovation, they walk out of the club hand-in-hand. I decide to stay put and take Collin's advice. There's nothing more I can do.

Chapter Thirteen

Experience—Part II

The thud of luggage dropping at my feet startles me.

"Am I still welcome or should I plan to hitchhike back to east Tennessee?"

"You look like shit. I bet you feel that way, too, huh?" I don't turn around to look at the face matching the very familiar voice.

"You know, I didn't screw Travis last night. We just kissed and messed around a little bit, he blathered on about you, and I left him on the bed, half-dressed and passed out cold. I want to put that on the table before you say yes or no to driving me home."

I offer Fielding a sly smile. "He's got a fantastic tool, doesn't he?"

"I am so glad you fuck-broke up with him, otherwise I would have never seen such a fantastic piece of man. But, I definitely won't be seeing him ever again." She fiddles with her luggage tag and frowns at me, pointing at the back of my SUV. "You never could pack a car worth a crap."

"Why aren't you going to see him again? It looked like he was into you at the club. You and Cliff are separated, and I don't care—too much." I cut my eyes back to her.

"Jenna. Number one, I'm married. And number two,

he's still in love with you."

"Oh, he is not. He was never in love with me. He never said he loved me, not one time."

"Well, the big dope wouldn't shut up about you! Even after I got him drunk he would *not* stop talking about you. Every time I thought I had the conversation turned, he'd find some way to turn it back. I do believe the boy's got it bad for you. Besides, I need time to get my shit together, and I can't do it humping someone else. Although, I'm sure he would be *so* good at it! But, the most important reason I didn't do anything else with him is because that would be really terrible. We're better friends than that."

"Fielding, I'm sorry—for everything. I'm sorry I haven't been here for you like I should have been. I've been selfish, and self-absorbed, and a really lousy friend. I'm sorry. I don't ever want to fight with you like that again because I need you too much, and you need me, even if you think you don't." I seal my apology with a solid punch to her arm.

Comforting her own bicep, she confesses, "Bitch, we're best friends. Nothing is going to change that. We're in this messy life together—being there *for* each other, as well as *with* each other. I've never thought that I didn't need you! In fact, I think I might need you more than I need anyone else, which is why I have slinked back, begging for a ride, and allowing you the opportunity to buy my friendship back with a delicious, nutritious breakfast."

"How about a dirty breakfast dive?"

"Absolutely! I hope I can keep it down. Tequila shots and making out with a twenty-something-year-old guy all night is hard on a cougar gal." She exhales deeply and shelters her eyes from the rising sun.

"Maybe we can share notes," I giggle, wrapping my arm around her, steadying her way, and just generally being there for her in case there's something I *can* do.

Chapter Fourteen

Some Things Only Come Around Once in Your Life…and What the Hell Is a MILF to Do About It?

This advice is worthy of repetition: In a world of extremes, it is amazing how a subtle difference can change the course of your whole life.

Subtle changes that can rock your whole world—for better or worse, depending on your stage in life: really awesome highlights, a minor fender bender with a very expensive car, sweet unsolicited praise from a stranger, getting your period before your first romantic getaway with a new guy, or being unexpectedly late for your period.

Fielding and I get together one Friday night for dinner at her new place—an apartment not far from campus. She lets on that she is happy in her newfound freedom, but I sense that there is some homesickness, too.

"You're quiet—everything okay?" I ask.

"Yeah, yeah, it's good. I miss the kids, though. It's hard coming home and not having them here, having everything be so quiet."

"You still see them after school, though, right?"

"Yeah, but it's the little things—seeing their little sleepy faces first thing in the morning, dinner conversation, bedtime. Those are the worst times, Jenna, the absolute worst." She wipes her eyes. "Sometimes, I don't know what the hell I'm doing."

"Are you and Cliff talking and still going to counseling?"

"Yeah, and I think we're making some good progress, but there's still a lot of work to do—a lot. How are things with Collin?"

"Good, so good in fact that I'm thinking of discussing *co-habitation*—maybe. I do like my own space, and the kids would have to be on board with it, too, of course. I don't know. Sometimes I think living together muddies the waters, know what I mean? You almost kill the passion with the *everyday* of life, but, that stuff can also pull you together."

"Tell me about it. There's just something so appealing about banging somebody and then sending him home."

My breath shudders and I let my body collapse onto Fielding's.

"Hey! Jenna! What's wrong? Honey, you don't *have* to bang someone and send him home if you don't want. You can always make him breakfast!" she jokes, but I don't laugh.

"I'm late. I am *late*. My period has been wacky the past couple of years—23 days, then 28 days, then 25 days— but I'm never *late* late! I don't know what to do!"

"Well, honey, yeah you do. You've done it three previous times. Take a pregnancy test. How late are you?"

Breathless and frantic I explain, "Well, I think about two weeks, maybe a few days over. I thought maybe being late was due to traveling to Kansas City, and the stress of Collin's competition, then Travis, and fighting with you! I blew it off."

"I thought you're on the Pill, right? And, you're using condoms—no way you can be pregnant."

"Well, I told Collin he didn't have to use condoms any longer because we're only having sex with each other and because he went and got a bunch of blood tests to show me he was no-rubber worthy."

Fielding grabs her side and laughs. "If nothing else he's thorough, but he cares about you, obviously. Still, I don't think you're pregnant—premenopausal maybe, but pregnant? It's highly unlikely."

"Right before we left for Kansas City, though, I was sick and couldn't keep a pill down. But took all the other ones right on time. So, don't you think that was probably enough to squelch a baby-making moment?"

"It probably was. We'll go get a pregnancy test and do it tonight. They're a lot more accurate now than they used to be."

"I brought one with me. Actually, I brought several with me. I wasn't sure which one was the best, so I bought three different kinds."

"You are such a Girl Scout! Well, start chugging the water. You've got a lot of pissing to do. Oh! This is just like in college!"

"Fielding, stop messing around. I'm scared!" I latch onto her sleeve. "I don't think I want another baby, not even if it's Collin's. What am I going to do?"

****

While I sit and wait on the test, I wonder, *How should I tell Collin if it's positive, or should I even tell him at all?* I could just take care of it and he would never have to know, but *I* would still know, and that could simply be the worst. After having had my kids, I'm not really sure I could do it, or take that pleasure away from him, even if the timing and the situation suck.

Fielding decides that it would be best to do all three tests with the same pee, so she finds an old glass beer stein and I pee in it. "Beer tastes like piss, anyway," she snorts. She's right, but I can't quite find as much humor in it as she does.

The latch on the bathroom door scares me witless, and my stomach is balled up in knots, ready to hear the news—no matter how good, or bad.

"Well, the good news is that all the results are the same, so I trust we've probably got an accurate result." Fielding's face is hollow, no expression whatsoever masks it.

"Okay. So, what's the bad news? Or is it bad?"

"Well, that depends on your perspective. Take a look for yourself." Fielding opens the door and sweeps me across into the bathroom.

On the counter are three white sticks—one with a familiar pink plus sign and two others that confirm what the first one indicates.

"Fielding, I'm pregnant!" I slink backwards, my back hitting the wall, and I sink to the floor.

Fielding picks me up off of the cold tile, a shaking, upset bag of nerves. "Jenna, a wise woman once gave me some terrific advice: Don't think of it as a crisis, think of it as a chrysalis. This could be your new beginning."

"Or, the beginning of the end," I whisper tearfully.

I know better.

There are some things that only come around once in your life—like an unplanned knock-up at age forty by a hot young stud—really hot and really young. Indeed, to hell with the past; I certainly do have a hell of a future ahead of me.

Chapter Fifteen

Baby, Oh Baby!

I'm wide awake.

I exhale, listening to Collin snore, wondering how I will tell him. How to tell him his life is about to change forever, to be as full of joy as any person could imagine, and how he'll know a lot of sorrow, and a lot of frustration, too. And then, there are things I can't really tell him; he'll have to discover those truths for himself.

The grandfather clock downstairs strikes three. Three o'clock in the morning. In a few short months, I may be up at three o'clock in the morning on a regular basis.

I roll to my side and cuddle up to Collin's back. His breathing is relaxed and rhythmic; it knows no stress or anxiety or weighty concerns. His emphasis is on himself, as it should be at this point of his life.

I bury my nose in his hair, trying, wanting to inhale some comfort. Reaching up, I trace his strong shoulders, letting my fingers meander around to his ribs. He is warm, and soft, and perfect.

For so many years in my marriage, I did not believe perfect was possible. In fact, I didn't believe I even deserved perfect. Collin will make a good father, not just for his child, but for my other children, too; much better than their real father could ever be inclined to do.

What worries me in telling Collin about being pregnant is not his response, and it's not whether he'll be inclined to make that part of his life as perfect as every other part, but whether he'll be inclined to stay and work to keep it together, even when things eventually unravel to a very *imperfect* point?

I close my eyes and reel off all the positive things I should be thinking about, instead of the negative realities that possess my mind at this hour. The glass is half full— but there's still no guarantee that it can't be knocked over and spilled.

Suddenly, Collin grabs my wrist and in a sleepy voice asks, "What's wrong? Why are you awake?" He strains his neck, moving his face closer to the clock. "Geez! What time is it anyway? I don't have my glasses.

"Uh, it's a little after three. I'm okay, just go back to sleep, sweetie." I murmur, rubbing his back, hoping he'll be groggy enough to find rest easily again.

"Well, is there something wrong? Why are you awake?"

"I'm a vampire."

"Are you going to bite me?" he laughs.

"Do you want me to?" I nibble on his ear lobe.

"Absolutely, then, we could be young and together forever. We would never die—and we would be obnoxiously rich. Vampires are the one percenters, you know, but zombies are definitely the other ninety-nine percent." He hiccups with laughter and I can only manage a weak smile, which dissolves in the darkness. He is completely unaware.

I choose my words carefully, aware of his leaden truth-ferreting gaze on me. Three a.m. pillow talk does not lend itself to heavy material like admitting an accidental pregnancy.

"Yeah, it would be nice to be young forever, *and* obnoxiously rich." I comb his chest hair with my fingertips, ignoring his pleading eyes.

"How long has this been going on, this sleeping issue? Maybe I need to check it out."

"Oh, no, I don't think so," I explain. "I'm fine, really. Sometimes, I just wake up. It's probably something I ate or drank, or something else."

"Something else like what?"

"Oh, I don't know. Sometimes I just wake up and think about all the stuff I have to do around the house, work things, the kids, money—normal things grown-ups sometimes think about."

"You shouldn't worry about those things. I can help you around the house. I'm not completely incompetent. Manual labor is not just the president of Mexico," he laughs, slipping his hands up and down the front of his face, now wide awake, too. "And, I think the kids like me well enough. You need me to help with homework again?"

"No, it's not that, unless you want to do it. I always appreciate your help, and I have to admit you really kicked some major ass on that algebra homework a few weeks ago."

He reaches over across the nightstand and turns on the lamp. "Is there something else? Something you think you can't tell me? Is Travis bothering you?" His annoyance at my truth-hedging underpins the insistence in his voice.

The truth—a soul-numbing, cardiac-inducing ménage of heart-breaking freedom, to which I obligated myself when I decided to be with Collin—or any version thereof that will buy me what I need, whatever that may be.

"No, not exactly. I was just thinking about him, about Travis. Sometimes I miss him, but it's not because I'd rather be with him, but because I'm afraid all of this will end, that I'll wake up from my fairy tale and it will be over, and I'll be alone, without you." It's not exactly the truth I need to tell him, but not exactly a lie either. "With Travis, I knew what the relationship was, and what it *wasn't*. The fling with him let me wade safely in the shallows. I didn't have to work to swim, or take a chance stepping into something unknown."

Collin sits up in bed, his face contorted as if I just sucker punched him in the stomach. "So, you want that back, that safe predictability? Would you rather be with Travis than with me?"

"No! No. Not at all. I just…I don't know what I need. I'm scared, Collin. I don't think I could be without you, not now, especially not now." I glance down at my stomach.

He takes my face in his hands and stares at me. I watch his lips slowly confess. "Would it help if I told you that I am falling completely, helplessly, and madly in love with you?"

His words pummel me. I am speechless from his percussion grenade admission—everything I want to hear and yet am afraid to know. Suddenly, it dawns on me: *Am I actually ready to jump feet first into such a commitment?*

The secret I am harboring inside of me, the secret that lives no matter how I decide to respond, is forcing my hand—and I don't like it one bit, even though my feelings for Collin remain unwavering. I'm not just hot for him anymore; I'm hotly *in love* with him, and I can't string him, or myself, along for any longer.

Fielding's words echo in my head, *Love is the most important thing.* "Collin, I love you. I love you, I love you, I love you." My lips seal the words along his jugular, all over his face, and any other place I can reach with my mouth.

He slides his warm body on top of mine—he doesn't ask; he doesn't have to ask. Lost in this lush forest of love, he rocks until he is inside of me and we repeat our love words again and again to each other. His strokes come slowly and we savor each one together. I raise my pelvis to rendezvous with his pumping—a spellbound, intoxicating liquor of lust that winds me up inside until I scream with satisfaction.

"Oh! I love when you make me come, baby! I love you so much!" I heave, my breath trying to keep pace with the flutter of my heart. My tongue finds his and we dissolve into a writhing, fevered hot mess.

"I love you, Jenna Craig," he whispers in my ear, flipping me to my knees. "And, I love making love to you every bit as much."

Riding the groove, he tugs me to him, whipping my hair to one side and licking my neck. Slowly, he builds my anticipation, his hand moving down between my breasts. He lingers on my nipples, forcing my arms above my head. Bending his neck around my shoulder, he kisses and licks my ear, his tongue climbing back down my neck. He gently pulls and rolls both nipples between his fingers, making me wetter with every second that passes, never missing a wickedly flaming hot, wet stroke.

Grabbing his hand I force him past my ribs. He

lingers on my stomach, rubbing circles on it. I hold my breath and suck in my gut, wondering whether he notices that anything is different. I quickly muscle his hand further down until it stops between my legs. He digs his fingers into my clit and a whole-body vibration overtakes me—both of us—and we collapse on the cool length of the bed.

The clock shows 4:30 a.m. Another chunk of time that I don't have to face the reality that threatens to deliver an unraveling deathblow to everything I have—and to everything I want.

At 6:30, the sun threatens my dreams, breaking in between the slats of the blinds. My stomach is queasy and I decide to go downstairs to fix breakfast. Collin is out cold. The only movement from his body is his chest rising and falling. I place my hand on him, hoping he'll wake soon. *Today has to be the day I tell him. I cannot deliver lies and expect to be dealt only the truth.*

Trying to remember what I ate with the other children when I was pregnant, I snatch an egg and the bread for toast. Between my mind's preoccupation and the clanging of pans, I don't hear Collin come into the kitchen. He swoops up behind me, cocooning his arms around me.

"Mmmm, your hair smells so good! I missed you when I woke up and you were gone. I was hoping we could have a replay of earlier—much earlier—this morning. Were you able to go back to sleep?"

"Yeah, you should bottle your boning powers for insomniacs. I slept like a—baby." My last word rattles me.

He laughs and blows my hair away from his face. "Well, baby, have you been up for very long?"

"No, I woke up about thirty minutes ago. The sun coming in through the window bothered me and I just decided to get up, get an early jump on breakfast. How about an egg and some toast?"

"How about I get *another* early jump on you and *then* we have breakfast? I'll help you cook it—dirty style." He grinds into my backside and kneads his hands into my soft belly. "Your stomach is so soft and sexy, yet toned. How do you keep it like that with all those naughty treats we've been enjoying? I don't care; keep it your own mystery, but don't change it. I love it!" He bends his head down and slowly, longingly kisses my stomach.

The truth is on the tip of my tongue, yet I swallow and force it back down—just until after breakfast. "Uh, well, a few days before our first date, the one in your dorm room, I had a procedure done. It uses radio frequency to heat up the fat under the skin and your lymphatic system clears it away." I bashfully look down at my toes feeling very foolish and stupidly vain. "After three kids via three cesareans I just decided it was time to feel good about my body again."

"Yeah, I've heard of that procedure, and it appears to be safe, but you didn't have to do that for me. I would have liked you however you are. Everyone has something odd or unusual; the human body is an anomaly. Have you ever seen my toes?"

Annoyed with his lack of understanding, I cut him off. "I didn't do it for you, Collin. I did it for me because I wanted to look a certain way—for *me*. You're probably too young and too male to understand." I wave him away.

Then, the ugly truth rears its head—up my throat

and out of my mouth. I stumble to the bathroom, Collin hot on my heels.

"Jenna! What's wrong? What the hell is going on with you? Are you okay? Is there something you're not telling me about your health? I think we need to go to the doctor for some tests!"

"Collin!" I yell "Please, just shut up and get a cold washcloth and some ice water, please? I'm sick. Please!"

He slinks out of the bathroom and I hear him take the stairs two at a time. Sinking to the floor, I sob. The cold tile is comforting and I wish I could be at home with my mother. Whenever I was little and sick she rubbed my back and stayed with me, making everything better. I close my eyes, nearly dozing, and hear footsteps. I feel a cold washcloth being draped across my forehead and warm hands caressing the small of my back. When I open my eyes, I realize it's not a dream.

Tearfully, I apologize. "I am so sorry. I've been a real asshole this morning, but I have a very good reason for it, although good is a relative term."

"What's wrong?" he asks, his eyes searching mine. "You know you can tell me—tell me *anything*, but please, don't lie to me. Don't think you have to protect me because I'm young. I can be strong enough for both of us. Don't you trust me enough to take care of you if you need it?"

"I'm pregnant. About eight or nine weeks."

He slides down the wall and sinks to the floor beside me, never making eye contact. "Are you sure? How did this happen? You told me you were on the Pill."

"I am on the Pill! I didn't plan this, trust me. Remember when I was sick right after we got back from your swim trials? I missed a pill, and I guess that was

142

enough. I've taken three pregnancy tests and I'm late—very late. I'm sure of it. I even had Fielding help me. We're kind of pros at this; between the two of us we have five kids."

"Fielding knew before *me*? Why didn't you come to me first?"

The male mind can be amazingly obtuse and dull, and it takes almost as much energy to explain why boyfriends and husbands will never replace girl-to-girl connections as the energy it takes to explain the truth in any matter.

"I was scared. And I thought you'd leave. I just have some serious decisions to make. Sometimes, it's easier to get things sorted in one brain before you bring in another."

"Except for Fielding, right?" he responds, anger stoking his tone.

"Please don't be mad at me about that. I've known Fielding for twenty years, and I've been with you for less than three months. Besides, I know you've been busy with applying for residencies. I didn't want to spoil your excitement."

"I'm a grown *man*, Jenna. When are you going to start treating me like one? Are you even sure it's mine?" A hurtful scowl creases his face.

This time, his words deliver a reciprocating sucker punch. "What the fuck is that supposed to mean? Are you asking in your own special *adult* way whether it might be Travis' baby?

"For your information, no, it's not. This is probably more than you deserve to know, but I always used condoms with Travis. I never trusted him like I trust you, but thanks for that vote of confidence. Besides, the timing would be all wrong for him. This is *your* baby, Collin." I put my face in my hands and the tears flow again. How could I even possibly consider having a baby with him, like this? "I love you, Collin, but this is obviously not going to work. I'll just deal with it myself. I'm used to that; why should it be any different now?"

Collin grabs a glass of water and steps out on the back deck. He settles into a chair and I watch him, considering the things he shared with me about his own childhood. His dad left his mom when he was nine. He essentially became an adult overnight; he looked after his little brother; he learned how to cook; he learned to be a man well before he should have had to. *So, why do I think that he'd treat his own child—or me—any differently? He doesn't need or want permission to be my man.*

I quietly walk outside and pull up a chaise beside him. "I don't want to leave things like this."

He pulls himself close to me and lays his head on my stomach. "Did you know that by ten weeks all the major organs are formed? The heart is functional at six weeks." Collin gently cups my stomach with both of his hands. "Six weeks—that's about how long it took me to realize that I loved you."

He tearfully kisses my belly "*Both* of you have my heart now."

Then he moves up to meet my eyes, my lips. "I am so sorry. I was an asshole just now. Please give me a chance to make this right. You're a great mom, Jenna, but I've already got one of those. What I need is a great *woman.* This is going to work between us because it's one of the best things that can happen to a man. Jenna, this time, it will be different for you. Please, you have to believe that this can work with me."

Collin suddenly jumps up and leaves me on the cold floor, alone. I hear his car unlock and he quickly scrambles back inside, his medical bag under his arm. "It's way too early to hear the heartbeat, but I want to try, anyway. Can I?"

As giant tears roll down my cheeks, I understand the man I love in a way that I never thought I could. He is young, and still has a lot to learn, but he wants to be a willing participant—in everything. People say that attitude is the biggest part of success. *Could it be that his sterling attitude is polishing the shitty dull finish right off of mine?*

He holds the stethoscope on my stomach, but shakes his head. "Ah, I knew it was too early to hear the baby's heartbeat, but I heard yours. And you know what else I heard?"

I shake my head, marveling at the excitement over his future—a very difficult future.

"I heard your stomach angrily growling. It's pissed. You need to eat. I think you spend so much time taking care of everyone else that you've forgotten you might need someone to take care of you for a change. How about you relax, and I'll cook breakfast?"

Wearily, I take his hand and follow him to the couch, and I let him take care of me.

Chapter Sixteen

Just Call Me Confidence

"Have you told him yet?" Fielding forgoes her usual hug and pleasantries, sliding into the booth right beside me at our new favorite lunch hang out—Noble Italian. Pizza is one of the few foods that is appealing to me, and that stays down.

"Yeah, I did."

"Well? What did he say? Look, dish girl, dish. Good grief! You made me wait all weekend to know. Besides, I've got to get back to work soon. The copier repairman is going to be there at one and he's super freaking hot." She shudders at the thought.

"He's happy, I think."

"I hate when you're pregnant. You're no fun. You're pukey," she laughs.

"Oh, piss on you! I'm doing the best I can. I'm too old for this."

"I read that getting pregnant late in life is a sign that you're going to live to be very old—maybe to one hundred. That's a plus." Fielding drapes her arm around me and gives me a squeeze. "What did he say?"

"Well, I didn't want to tell him, and he knew something was up. So, *after* I puked, I had to tell him. At first, he was upset that I told you *before* him and then he asked if it was his!"

"What a son-of-a-bitch! Did you throw him out? Little bastard, when I see him again—"

"No, no. I didn't throw him out. I assured him it was his, and not Travis'. We haven't been together that long so I guess it was a fair question."

Fielding interrupts me, ducking her head beneath the eye line of the back of the booth. "It isn't Travis' is it?"

"No! What kind of dishonest, stupid slut do you two think I am?"

"Aw, don't take it personally. I watch too much Jerry Springer. I just needed to ask. You know I can't let a question go."

"He ultimately ended up apologizing and he said it was one of the best things that could happen to a man. Before he made me breakfast, he got his stethoscope to see whether he could hear the baby's heartbeat, but it was too soon."

Fielding's eyes fill up and nearly pour over down her chipmunk cheeks full of a garlic breadstick. "Okay, he's not a bastard and I won't say a word to him, except for thank you for being so good to my best friend in the world who totally deserves a good guy. Jenna, I'm really happy for you."

"Yeah, I wish I could be as happy. It's just such a shock. And, the worst part is that he doesn't know how difficult this next year is going to be. What if he bails on me?"

Fielding takes the pizza cutter and mauls an unsuspecting piece of our pie. "Then we will find him, and we will hurt him—zip off the old penis. He won't, though. I have a feeling everything is going to be alright with this one. He's trainable if nothing else."

I drop my head into my hands, laughing. "You're

awesome, but I feel like hell. I'm getting up at the butt crack of dawn to eat so that I can go to work. By the way, did you know that there is porn on at like four in the morning?"

"Yeah, honey, everyone knows that—Skinemax."

"I don't like the soft-core stuff. It's too confusing. I keep trying to figure out whether they're actually doing it or grinding and pretending. It's pretty titillating, though. I think Collin and I have had sex every morning this week."

"Well, bragger! I'll bet he likes that!"

I study her face and know that she's not just here for me, but always here with me. "Thanks, Fielding. For everything."

She throws her hands out at me. "Oh, shut up! You know I love you—knocked up or not. I guess this means that you won't need a ride to the abortion clinic?" she asks, fake punching me in the stomach.

"Yeah, I think I'm good," I laugh, shaking my head at her. "I'll see you at Rafferty's for Collin's residency party?"

"I wouldn't miss it for the world."

****

"Wow! This is amazing. I can't believe you did all of this—for *me*." Collin's mouth gapes open and he reaches up to get a balloon.

"Well, it's a big deal! You got the residency you wanted at the best hospital in Knoxville, maybe in all of Tennessee. That's worth celebrating."

He lowers his head and aims his eyes right at me; it's the stare, the look that hooked me the first time, the look that sends my panties straight to the floor with absolutely no second thoughts or arguments or excuses.

"Have I ever told you how absolutely gorgeous and wonderful I think you are?"

Licking my lips, I warn him, "If you don't stop that we'll have to lock ourselves in a bathroom stall, or find an unoccupied corner." I press my newly inflated tits up against him, grinding into his leg. "Wow! Is that a tongue depressor in your pocket or are you just happy to see me?"

Collin holds up his hands to get our guests' attention. He turns to me, taking my hands in his, and lowers himself down on one knee. "Jenna, you have come to mean everything to me, and I know the timing on certain things is not perfect, but I guess I'm just an old-fashioned guy. There's nothing I want more than for you to call me your husband, and for me to call you my wife." He struggles to release a small, bulky box from his pocket. "I love you. Will you marry me?"

Fielding's voice jumps out of the crowd. "Jenna! Look at the ring! It's gorgeous!"

A silver antique ring with a bezel set sapphire surrounded with pavé diamonds takes my breath away. In college Fielding and I coveted and sketched mental images of this ring as we sat in the cafeteria planning our dream weddings—without a solitary man on the horizon. It was the epitome of hope. The epitome of confidence.

"I'm sorry I knew before you did!" Fielding announces, her hands cupped around her mouth, hopping up and down on her heels behind Collin, smacking him on the back. "Now we're even!"

I've spent the better part of a decade worrying about every decision I've made, drowning myself in the "what ifs." *Is it wrong? Is it right? What will people think? Who will be happy, mad, sad, upset? What if I start looking old and he leaves? What if the baby doesn't bring us together, but grows us apart? What if this whole marriage thing doesn't work...again?*

Maybe as women we're conditioned to think that way. *What if, though, he's the love of my life, the one I've been waiting for? What if we make it, against all the odds? What if this is the beginning of a wonderful, beautiful dream?*

What I have finally learned is that people will think what they want: they will feel how they feel, regardless of my decisions. I have to put myself first sometimes, and be confident that it's the right decision for me...just because it is. I don't need to explain or defend. Reframe my fears and walk away—no shits given to the wind. There's confidence in not giving a damn sometimes.

I study the smiling, happy faces in the crowd—my children, Collin's friends and his parents, my friends and parents. I have come full circle. I am renewed. I am revived. I am finally *loving* my experience, and confident that I *deserve* it.

Fielding's words pop and spin in my head as I turn Collin's question over in my mind. *Jenna, sometimes with love, you just gotta say fuck it.*

Some people might think I've totally lost it, thinking I can make this work.

Call me a dreamer, I guess. But...don't call me crazy for wanting the fairy tale: don't call me a desperate middle-aged woman because I went for the young guy, and don't call me hopeless because I'm giving love another shot.

Just call me confidence...because that's all I've got that's really all *mine.*

My palms are clammy and there's the proverbial

lump in my throat. I'm pretty sure my heartbeat is jackhammer-heavy, but I've never been more sure of anything, and scared to death at the same time of this lovely, unexpected turn my life has taken. *Well, today, right now, in this moment, I'm going to honor my life, honor myself, and say, 'fuck it.'*

"I love you, too, Collin. Yes, I will absolutely marry you!"

A word about the author…

Stella Grae is an unassuming English professor, copyeditor, and copywriter living in Lexington, Kentucky. She's the author of the short story "Power Play" that was originally published in the website erotica journal Oysters and Chocolate. In her spare time she enjoys sipping on bourbon, nibbling cheesy grits, and philosophizing about love and sex in her blog, "Bone Up," which can be found on her website: stellagraeerotica.weebly.com…along with other sexy tidbits. This is her first erotica novel.

stellagraeerotica.weebly.com

Thank you for purchasing
this publication of The Wild Rose Press, Inc.

For questions or more information
contact us at
info@thewildrosepress.com.

The Wild Rose Press, Inc.
www.thewildrosepress.com